PRAISE FOR

"*Oracle is a fantastic read. It had me from page one and a real page turner...*"

— S. JOESTEN

"*Jaw Dropping!*"

— AMAZON REVIEWER

"*I'd recommend it to anyone who enjoys mystery, psychics, and Greek mythology.*"

— JULIE WEEKS

"*It didn't take long for me to become invested in the story with Diana the main character, it hit the ground running and I was hooked.*"

— PAMELA MCK

"*Almost a scarily good book.*"

— AMAZON REVIEWER

*To all of us who have made it through this pandemic and lived
to tell about it, this book is for you.*

AMENDS

A DIANA HAWTHORNE PSYCHIC MYSTERY

CARISSA ANDREWS

THE ORACLE OF DEAD GODS

*T*HERE'S NO WAY IN HELL I'm allowing them to trap me here.

I shiver from the cold sweats brought on by this morning's vision. They're coming at me now with more frequency. *More urgency.*

That's why I had to get out of the hotel room and go back to the source. I needed to sit inside the vibrations of the temple again, just to be sure.

Luckily, the Temple of Apollo isn't more than a few minutes from where we're staying.

I bite my lower lip and clutch the steering wheel tightly.

I'm almost positive I know what the visions mean, but I'm not sure how to lean into them. Not when I'm so close to having everything I've ever wanted.

My jaw clenches and I cast a gaze over my shoulder. Blake's soft breathing pulses up and down softly like a metronome to my very existence. He has no idea what awaits.

There's movement in the energy around this space. It feels like the old gods are preparing their return and I've become the linchpin to their plan.

Too bad for them, though. I've come too far to sit on a pile of rubble, telling fortunes to the rich and powerful while they rouse the troops. Because let's face it, once word gets out that the Oracle of Delphi has returned, those in power will come for me the way they did before. Humanity hasn't changed all that much.

Plus, with the advent of social media, I shudder to think how quickly the information will travel. I'll become a spectacle—*some sort of dancing monkey*—and the privacy I've come to know and love will be lost.

Then, rather than being accessible to all the poor, sad souls of the world, I'll be fashioned into a weapon. One they can use to their advantage.

Then, the fanatics will come.

First, they'll try to kill me. But when they find out they can't, a worse fate will come. I'd probably be locked in a vault under the Vatican somewhere with everything else that scares the hell out of the mundanes of the world.

Fuck that.

I practically growl, shuddering at the thought.

It's bad enough I have to be an oracle for dead and buried gods. I should at least be able to pick and choose where I go and how I serve.

Come on, Apollo. Give me at least that much.

Swallowing hard, I put the rental car into park. I leave it running and slip out into the cool morning air. As gently as I can, I close the driver's side door and peer inside. Blake's hands are pinned by his arms and his dark

2

eyelashes flutter under the weight of his dreams. Hopefully, they're better than mine.

I don't fully understand why he wanted to come with me. It's not like he's a morning person. He could still be warm and comfortable in the hotel bedroom. I know that's where I'd rather be.

My heart flutters and I can't help but smile.

Turning around, the wind whips my hair in a cyclone around my head. It's a dazzling display with varying strands of gold and pink as the rising sun bleeds its welcome into my hair.

Despite all of this, I reach for the ponytail holder in my pocket and tie my hair back. I need to be focused and centered now. Taking my time, I meander the trail to the ruins of the Temple of Apollo.

It's been two days since the arrest of Lester and his cronies. Two days since I got my memories back.

Two days since I gave up a mortal life to continue on with the insanity of this supernatural, immortal one.

When I reach the ruins, I take a seat on a stone wall and sigh.

It's also been two days since my soul mate was returned to me.

Blake is so excited to be uncovering our past, one memory at a time. His life as Anastasios was just as locked to him as my past was to me. At least we have that much in common.

But this undercurrent of anxiety clouds my elation.

I exhale a jagged breath and settle into the energy of the space. My gaze lifts, settling on the horizon. At this time of the morning, the view is almost the same as it was millennia ago. However, the beauty does nothing to shake the terrible revelation that while I have regained so much, my life is no longer my own.

While not exactly the most idyllic of circumstances, the past two millenniums have molded me into the woman I've become. How the hell am I meant to revert to someone I no longer am?

That woman was shed a long, long time ago.

This never-ending existence has left me jaded. Sure, I might be more of a prickly pear these days, but I'd also like to think the rougher edges have left me with a little more depth. And certainly a little wiser to the world as a whole.

Being psychic can only get you so far. You still need experience to accurately unpack everything.

Inhaling deeply, the crisp morning air clings to my lungs until I exhale the breath in a soft plume of frozen water droplets. I lean forward, placing my elbows on my knees. Bringing my hands to prayer position, I press the edge of my index fingers to my lips in an effort to silence my mind.

Blake may be recalling bits and pieces of our past life together, but he doesn't remember everything. He doesn't have the recollection of all of his past lifetimes, and I'm not sure what to make of that. Maybe it's a byproduct of me meddling with our memories. As long as he's happy with what he remembers, maybe that's all that matters.

My one concern is that he doesn't understand the restraints I now wear, and all for the sake of saving him. If he knew what I gave up to do it, he'd call me a damn fool.

But then again, he doesn't know all that I've endured without him by my side.

There have been so many decisions I've made that would shock him. So much I've seen and done that I'm not proud of throughout these years alone. Rather than being set on a course and following it to its destination, my life has been a tangle of events that would leave others crawling out of their skin.

Maybe even Blake.

And it's certainly something the gods could use against me if they really wanted.

My stomach constricts and I swallow back my uneasiness.

I'll cross that bridge when—*or if*—it ever comes.

For now, though, I need to find a loophole to this prison sentence before it becomes my reality.

As much as I love the memories of growing up here, and the time of being with Anastasios, I no longer have any desire to live in Greece. That time has passed. Sorrow lingers here like a layer of fog that won't dissipate. I can feel it now, even as I sit here.

This is where everything went wrong... Where two-thousand plus years of self-loathing began.

No, I don't want to be stuck here. Blake and I found each other again in Helena. It's where we belong now. Besides, it's not like he'll want to uproot Aiden and his entire life to move to Greece.

Arms wrap around my neck from behind, making me jump. Not an easy feat, all things considered.

"Didn't mean to startle you." Blake's words are gruff, but hold a smile at the edges of his tone. His thoughts tumble through various things to say, but they're garbled by the early morning. One thing is clear, though...he's amused that he caught me off guard. He kisses the top of my head and takes a seat beside me on the bench. "At least it's easy to find you. You're always in the same place."

My lips twitch, but don't fully form into a smile.

"Uh oh. What's wrong?" he asks. His eyebrows draw down, darkening his features as he puts on his investigator hat.

I straighten my shoulders and shake off my apprehension. There's no point in worrying him until I have a plan.

"Nothing," I mutter.

The creases around his brown eyes deepen and he grunts. "Mhm."

Shaking my head, I stand up and stretch nonchalantly. "No, seriously. It's nothing to worry about."

"Then why won't you tell me what's going on?" he asks, arching an eyebrow.

I press my lips tight and give him a knowing look. "Because it's nothing to worry about. I've just got a lot on my mind. We've been through hell and back these past few weeks."

His expression is tight and he refuses to remove me from underneath his scrutiny. I hold firm, trying to lighten the energy between us.

Finally, he leans back a bit and says, "Yeah, if you would have told me a month ago that I'd be having past-life memories about being married to the Oracle of Delphi, or that I've made a pact with the god Apollo, I would have said to lay off the acid."

I chuckle, dropping my gaze to the sandy ground. "Right?"

So much has changed.

A little over a month ago, I had been trying desperately to understand my past. If I'm completely honest, I don't think I expected anything to come of it. After being let down time and time again, how could I?

But the Violet Flame invocation came through.

Demetri came through.

My stomach constricts again and a fresh wave of guilt and anxiety rolls through me. I exhale, trying to release the tension. Instead, the realization that I'm the reason Demetri's powers were stripped from him punches me in the feels.

His powers are gone and mine have grown. Oh, he'll *love* that.

Again, I press my fingertips to my mouth and turn away from Blake.

"See, now I know something's up. What's going on with you?" Blake says as he presses his hand against my back, letting me feel his presence.

He's genuinely concerned for me. I can sense it in every molecule of his being. But I've been alone so long, I don't quite know how to open up completely. Even him.

He's fragile and human…and I could still push him away if I'm not careful.

I close my eyes for a moment, allowing my abilities to survey the landscape of our new relationship before proceeding. "When you mentioned where we were at a month ago, it got me thinking about what was happening in my life around that time… I'm just worried about a friend back home," I admit, hoping it will be enough for him to let things go.

"Is something wrong with him?" he asks, narrowing his gaze.

My eyebrows pull in as I try to put things into the right words. It's way easier when I'm just the vessel, delivering universal information. But when I'm at the center of it all, shit gets so damn complicated and messy.

"You could say that. Yeah. He was helping me with a ritual and it backfired." I shake my head. "Well, sort of."

Blake continues to watch me, giving me the space to process through what I want to say without interruption. It's who he is—*the watcher*. It's why he's such a good private investigator.

I inhale slowly and let my shoulders drop. "He's psychic as well, but after the ritual, the blowback cost him his gifts. I don't think he's very happy with me."

"Is there anything that can be done?" Blake asks, switching gears into fixer mode.

I shrug. "Honestly, I don't know."

"Well, I fully admit that I'm new to this whole supernatural thing, so correct me if I have this wrong," Blake begins, clearing his throat softly, "but you're connected to some pretty powerful beings. I'd be surprised if you can't pull a few strings for him."

I mull over his words for a moment. Would the gods help Demetri? I suppose they could, but then it would be one more thing they could hold over me. If they even felt it was something to bother with. Who knows with gods and their plans?

I glance at Blake, then back out over the valley. "While technically true, the gods don't look kindly on trivial requests. I should know. And this…*would definitely be considered trivial.*" Besides that, in a way, it's a direct consequence of my selfishness all those years ago. It's serving not only to punish him—*but me.* And maybe I should be punished.

"Well, I have faith in you. If there's a way to fix this for him, you'll figure it out. So, stop worrying, would you?" Blake says, grabbing hold of my arms and spinning me to face him. He lifts his right hand to my cheek, brushing back a strand of pink hair that's slipped loose from my ponytail.

I inhale sharply, suddenly tuned into every movement he makes and the proximity of his body to mine. While we may have been married in a past life, everything about this relationship we have now is so new. I can count the times we've kissed on one hand…and that's as far as we've taken things.

I've had relationships in the past that existed solely for sweaty entanglements—and nothing else. No names, no shared experiences beyond that. *But this...*

Blake's eyes linger on mine, holding my gaze so long my heart begins to race.

Can he see into my soul? Can he feel my thoughts?

My breath catches and I try to shake this horrible feeling niggling its way into my consciousness. Love is a beautiful, strange thing. I love him so deeply, even though we've barely met in this new lifetime. His essence is the same.

Yet, I've changed so much.

What if after all these years, he finds out I'm no longer worthy of his love?

Those worries puddle at my feet when Blake slowly bends in, brushing his lips against mine. The whiskers in his peppered goatee tickle the edges of my lips, making my skin hum.

As much as I try to steer clear of reading his thoughts, they still come to me with fervor. Despite his gentleness, he wants the exact same thing I want. Only, he's just as nervous to reach for it as I am.

I lean into his kiss, wrapping my arms around his neck, and entangling my fingers into his dark locks. The wind whips around us, echoing through the branches nearby and the ruins themselves. Hidden in the undercurrent of the breeze, I swear I can hear someone calling my name.

Only, it's not my name anymore...

The Grecian accent is thick, but my mind translates them instantly."Amarantham? Is that you?"

I wish I could tell you the past never comes back to haunt you...but I'd be lying.

As I spin around, I stare straight into its gleaming brown eyes.

STARING INTO THE FACE OF
ANCIENT HISTORY

"**K**YROS?" I say, dropping my hands from Blake and taking a confused step back. "Is that you?"

The ages are peeled back like the pages of a calendar as my shattered mind tries to comprehend what I'm seeing. Somehow, though I have no idea how... I'm staring into the elderly gaze of my former assistant.

From like, *two millennia ago.*

And if this old man is Kyros, one thing's for certain, time has not been kind. His once thick, dark hair that curled around his ears and framed his face is stringy and devoid of its former color. In its place is lusterless gray strands that barely manage to cover the shape of his scalp. His former distinguished stature is also diminished to a sideways hunch as if his spine has given in to the demands of time.

Yet, even with all of this, even without my psychic abilities... I'd know those olive-green eyes anywhere.

Blake throws me a befuddled glance, then eyes Kyros

with the same discerning suspicion he'd give a suspect. Thankfully, he keeps his mouth shut, even if his mind is threatening to barrage me with its cacophony. I put up a mental block, tuning him out as I try to settle into the situation.

My gifts are annoyingly silent about the how and why he could be here. What an excellent time to take a little vacation.

Kyros observes Blake in the same regard, his weathered face scrunching with an incredulity I've only ever witnessed on Renaldo's face.

"It would appear to be the case, yes," he replies.

I marvel for a moment at the way his words flow out of his mouth in Greek but translate into modern-day English inside my mind. I haven't spoken the old language for what feels like eons.

Brains are so weird. Or maybe it's just my brain? Eh, who knows?

I shake my head, trying to knock away the cobwebs and disorientation. "But…*how?*"

Apparently, complete sentences are failing me now.

Excellent. This bodes well.

"I have some ideas. However, it was but a few days ago when I became aware of a return to this…*existence*," he says, suggesting toward his being. His lips press tightly as he shoots a sideways glance at Blake.

Who is the gentleman? Kyros's thoughts reach out, entering my mind in with the two-way communication link only he and I have ever shared.

Obviously, he isn't certain how openly he can speak

with a stranger beside us. Only, Blake's no stranger at all. Not to either of us.

I glance over to Blake, then double-take, thanks to the look on his face. Despite myself, I laugh out loud. His expression is tight and he looks like an infant who'd been given a bit of lemon for the first time.

If it's even possible, his eyebrows lower further.

Covering up my case of the giggles, I clear my throat, and I extend a hand out toward Kyros. "Blake, this...*is Kyros.* He's—" Again, words escape me and I struggle to explain something that makes zero sense in my brain. "He's..."

A sparkle of recognition lights behind Blake's eyes and his features soften. "Kyros?" he whispers. "Why do I remember that name?"

Kyros snorts, mumbling under his breath something about "how he very much doubted that."

I marvel for a moment that he was able to understand Blake. Perhaps it's not just my weird brain, after all. Then again, he always had a knack for understanding the language of those who wanted to see me. Besides his psychic link to me, it was sort of his gift and it kept out the...

"Ahhhh..." I mutter, tipping my chin upward as realization slaps me upside the head. "I should have known..."

This is Apollo's doing.

He's brought back Kyros as a way to settle me back into my role.

I inhale sharply.

So, it begins.

Both of the men turn their expectant gaze toward me.

13

"Apollo's brought you back," I state, matter-of-factly as I turn to face Kyros.

His weary features tighten and he crosses his arms over his chest wrinkling the fabric of his old-school tunic. "Well, that was fairly obvious, do you not think? Have you lost your edge, Amarantham?"

I snicker. Lost my *mind*, maybe. But he has yet to see just how sharp my edge can be.

Extending a hand out between us, I shake my head. "Please, don't call me that. That woman is dead and buried. You've been gone for a fair few years, Kyros. I go by Diana now."

Kyros's left eyebrow twitches, evidently trying to decide on its own accord whether or not to raise. The war is lost though when it gives out and barely arches.

"Would someone please explain what in the hell is happening? Should I be worried?" Blake says, clearly annoyed by the lack of information.

"Who exactly is this?" Kyros asks, maintaining steady eye contact and tipping his head toward Blake.

"Who am I? Who the hell are you? What in the hell is happening?" Blake's tone is fierce as he jabs a finger toward Kyros. Clearly, his brain can translate, too.

Or is Kyros somehow speaking English now? Gods, I can't tell anymore.

Either way, another point for magic.

Without allowing me to respond, Kyros steps up into his space, clearly not afraid of Blake's bravado. He shoves his gnarly fingers into Blake's mouth, prying his lips apart and taking a good look inside. With a harumph, he moves on to his eyes, planting his thumb and index finger on opposite lids to pry them open.

"What in the actual f—" Blake begins, tearing himself away from the old man's clutches.

"Anastasios?" Kryos breathes, clearly having winded himself with his exertion.

Blake shoots me a look that puts his previous bewilderment to shame.

Ignoring it, I take a step toward Kyros. "You can tell he's Anastasios?"

Kyros attempts to clasp his hand behind his back but gives up when he can't quite get his hands to connect. "Erm, yes. It is a bit obvious, is it not?"

I scrunch my face. I don't know how obvious it is just by looking at him.

"Very well. I approve," Kyros says, straightening his shoulders and tipping his head in some sort of gesture of approval.

"Well, gee, I'm so glad we have your blessing," I say, rolling my eyes so far I'm pretty sure I see the back of my skull. "Look, as happy as I am to see you, I think Apollo wasted his time."

Kyros gapes at me.

"A lot's happened and well, I'm not so sure I want to play oracle to a city of dead gods anymore," I say, verbalizing the feelings that have been crowding my head.

Kyros tsks. "Amaranth—"

"Diana," I correct before he can go any further.

"Diana," he says with a hint of agitation, "you have a job to attend to. Your role is far more important than simply… What did you call it? 'Playing oracle'?"

"Does someone want to explain to me what's happening here?" Blake says, breaking into the conversation. "Because as much as I can follow the crazy train, I'm still a little lost."

"Amar…*Diana* needs to resume her post," Kyros says, matter-of-factly. His wrinkled features twitch with a certain amount of pride for being in the know, despite looking like the Crypt Keeper.

"Resume her post? As in…*here?*" Blake says, turning to face me.

I wince, knowing my lack of communication is about to take a good chunk out of my backside. "Maybe? No?" I sigh, running my hands through my hair and walking away. "Look, I don't know. All of this is new to me. I don't know what's expected of me just yet. I'm trying to get a read on the situation, but the universe is being aggravatingly bipolar on the matter. Which is fine by me because, to be frank, I'm not real keen on being told what to do."

"But that's what he's on about, right? You're meant to resume your role?" Blake says, his brown eyes darkening.

"It would appear," I say, my shoulders sagging.

"Well, how in the hell is that meant to work, Diana?" he asks, voicing the same concerns that have been plaguing me.

"It is very simple. She claims her rightful place and continues her work in the name of Apollo," Kyros says. "From what I can sense of things, this world is in dire need of a champion."

"Oh, you have noooo idea," I say, both in sarcasm and complete conviction. It needs a champion all right. That doesn't mean it has anything to do with me.

"Look, there's a lot to unpack here. Anytime now, this place is going to be flooded with tourists. Maybe we should take Aristotle here back to the hotel and continue our conversation there," Blake says, checking the time.

"Aristotle," Kyros huffs. "That pompous blowhard is of no relation."

Blake gives him a side-eye and turns his gaze to me.

"Yeah, okay. Let's go…" I say, wiping my fingertips across my forehead.

Without waiting for additional permission, Blake grabs hold of my hand and spins on his heel. He marches us past Kyros and down toward the car. Kyros trails after us, trying his best to keep up, but his ancient frame isn't used to the rocky pathways and mountainside. Probably because it's been recently resurrected and half of it still thinks it's part of the landscape.

When we reach the parking lot, he nearly has a heart attack and dies for the second time.

"What in the graces of the gods is that monstrosity?" he asks, raising a bony finger toward the rental car as Blake and I open our doors.

I chuckle under my breath, wishing I could see the world through his eyes. It has to be a bit unnerving coming into the modern era from so long ago. But also pretty miraculous.

"Just get in, gramps," Blake says, clearly not as amused as I am.

I wave Kyros toward us and I'm barraged by the sense of fear rolling off him in waves.

Blake on the other hand is a ball of conflicting thoughts and feelings. I try not to pry into his mind as he works through all of this. I can't say I blame him for being a bit freaked out. We've left the land of the ordinary and entered the realm of the extraordinary. There's bound to be a few mental hiccups in the transition.

Spinning around, I open the back door and point inside. "Just sit. You're going to love this."

Kyros's eyes narrow. "I sincerely doubt that."

Blake slams his palm into the center of the steering wheel, blasting the horn. Kyros nearly jumps out of his skin and scurries over to where I'm pointing. Without another word, he hops inside and takes a seat, tugging his tunic around his legs as he does so.

Shaking my head, I look up to the sky, then close his door. "Gods help me."

Taking a deep, cleansing breath, I return to the passenger seat and hop in.

An air of agitation has settled inside the vehicle and I don't dare try to lighten the mood. Not yet. As accepting as Blake has been about all of this, he's still new to it, too. I have to remember that.

Kyros whimpers from the backseat as Blake puts the car into reverse. "What kind of sorcery…" he mutters under his breath.

The short drive back to the hotel is a tense one. Each of us is a live wire that could be set off with a single touch. So, best not to tempt fate.

When we get inside, I head straight to the small bar on the counter and pour a drink for each of us. Blake shakes his head, pushing the glass of whiskey back onto the counter. Kyros takes his glass, giving it a good sniff before downing the contents in one big gulp. His eyes nearly fall out of his head, but he holds his hand out for another.

Snorting to myself, I pour him some more and down the contents in my glass.

"All right, guys, here's what's going to happen. I need time to process all of this. I'm not prepared to take on the mantle of *Oracle* again. At least, not without some proper internal debate and self-flagellation." I grab Blake's glass and down the contents of his as well.

"But what about Helena? About us?" Blake leans in and he whispers urgently in my ear.

I look into his desperate eyes and my decision is nudged one step closer toward abandonment of my post.

My tongue grazes my lower lip as I try to find the words. "I know, Blake. I know. And I'm right there with you. But I also know I can't take this lightly. These are *gods* we're talking about."

"Then where is he? Why send Kyros?" Blake sputters, pointing at Kyros.

Kyros glances up at the mention of his name, just as he tentatively sits down on the edge of the bed. Then, after a second, starts bouncing up and down.

I lower my eyebrows and shake away the absurdity. "How the hell do I know? It's all problematic, isn't it? I mean, if I were a god—"

Suddenly, as if called forth, Apollo's voice booms from Kyros's fragile body, echoing with the kind of power only a god can manifest. My mouth snaps shut.

"Pythia, do not question your responsibilities now. Your oath binds you to me and the time is coming for my return," he says.

I round on Kyros, my hands balled into fists as I come back to myself. "And what about me? What about *my* life?"

"You've had millennia to entertain a life of your own. Now, it is time to deliver upon your promises," Kyros says, his back rigid and eyes glassed over with a lavender glowing light.

I shake my head. "No, that's not even fair. I've just gotten Anastasios back."

"That was a consequence of your own doing."

"It doesn't make it any less true. I want time with him," I fire back. "I *need* time."

"The rules still apply. Your soul mate will follow you through the ages. This version of him is of no consequence to the grand design," Kyros says, his voice still resonating with the kind of vibrato that would make others cower.

I clench my teeth and curse under my breath.

"But—" I begin, but my mouth is once again snapped shut. Agitation swells in my gut. I hate being controlled like that.

"You have until the rise of the next full moon to begin your duties," Apollo says. He doesn't stick around for the rebuttal I was gonna shove straight up his ass. Kyros's body goes somewhat limp and he shudders away the possession.

"Screw this," I say, fighting the urge to strangle Kyros just for having the nerve to be a vessel for Apollo.

"Amar—Diana. You know you cannot shirk your responsibilities. Why must you fight this?" Kyros asks, clutching at the front of his tunic like he might keel over from a heart attack at any moment.

"Because it's not my choice, is it?" I lament.

"I believe we are all here by a design not of our choice," Kyros offers.

True or not, it doesn't help.

"No, screw this. *Screw this.* If Apollo wants me to be his oracle so badly, he'll need to do better than sending me idle threats and a *geriatric* assistant," I spit, jabbing a finger at Kyros.

Kyros simply shrugs at the description. "Fair."

"No, you know what?" I say, my resolve hardening. "I've come too far to be anyone's pawn—*Apollo's included.* So, I'm throwing in the towel. *I'm out.* Time to make my life my own for a damn change."

I throw my hands up in the air and walk out of the small hotel room, leaving the two men standing awkwardly together.

I should feel bad. My gifts should be guiding me back to the temple. Hell, I should feel like I've made a mistake. *But I don't.*

I take that as a sign. I mean, hell, what's the worst that could happen?

3

FREEDOM FIGHT

"*I*f you are planning on leaving this godforsaken place, then I am coming with you," Kyros says, hobbling after me. Determination filters into his tone as he tugs at the neck of his new shirt, clearly uncomfortable by their confines. "There's nothing left for me here, Amaran—*Diana*."

I pat him on the arm the way you would when a kid hands you a drawing and you have to tell them it looks fantastic. But in reality, you can barely tell if it's a person or a black hole.

"That means you're free, Kyros. You're not beholden to anyone but yourself. Consider yourself officially relieved of your duties to the Oracle. Go live your life. Explore the world. So much of it has changed. Live a little," I say, patting him on the shoulder as I walk back to the small dresser tucked in the corner of the hotel room. I grab the remainder of my clothes and return to the open suitcase that's splayed open on the bed.

Kyros lowers his eyebrows and his lips transform into

prunes with his tight frown. "Amarantham, you and I both know Apollo will not approve of this way of thinking. It's a foolish errand to even believe you can outwit him. For reasons unknown to me, he chose to resurrect me, and I highly doubt he'll let that go without a proper fight."

I chew on my lower lip. Kyros is right, but at the same time, what's Apollo gonna do? It's not as if he'll kill Kyros if he needs him. He'd simply snap his fingers and put him back into the aether if he's not successful with his mission. Kyros would be none the wiser and in all honesty, probably plenty happier for it.

I'm doing him a favor by trying to set him free. At least he'll get something I'll never have. *Freedom*.

Blake walks back into the hotel room from outside. He tucks his phone into his back pocket and catches my eye. "Our flight is confirmed and we're checked in. Are you ready?"

I nod. "Yeah, I just need to get Kyros squared away." I unzip the top zipper and pull out the envelope I put together for him. It took a little doing and a bit of tech magic from Aiden, but Kyros will be taken care of. I even have people ready to keep an eye on him and help him through this transition.

Kyros narrows his gaze, watching my movements as if I'm about to off him. Yet, he doesn't make a move to rise from the comfort of the bed's edge, so he must not be overly concerned.

Holding the envelope to my chest for a beat, I exhale slowly and hand it over to him. "Here. This has everything you'll need to start a new life."

Kyros narrows his eyes and rips open the envelope.

"We've paid for the hotel room for the next month, so don't feel like you have to hurry. But that should be enough money to get you situated. And if you need anything, you can always call me. We'll take care of you," I say, my words tumbling out fast before I lose my nerve.

I feel absolutely terrible for wanting to leave him, but I'm also terrified for what it would mean to Apollo by having him come with us.

Kyros plucks out the passport and credit cards. "What in all of Tartarus are these?" He flips through the pages of the passport, his forehead creased.

"You'll need them for traveling. Well, assuming you want to get beyond the borders of Greece. This one is for flying or crossing into another country," I say, pointing at the passport. No need to worry him that they're high-end forgeries. "This one is for paying for stuff."

His features tighten. "What of this?" He pulls out the remaining wad of cash we had on hand. "Is this not for *paying for stuff*?"

"Of course it is. It's just not as much as what's on the card," I say.

His eyes widen as he raises his hand and places the card under his scrutiny. "Astounding."

Blake huffs over my shoulder.

Reaching back into the suitcase pocket, I hand over the cellphone Blake purchased last night when Kyros was snoring up a storm. "This will help you keep in touch. I've already plugged in my number, in case you need to reach me." I press through the menu options and show him how to dial me up. "I wish I had more time to show you how it works, but…" I point back to Blake, "we have a flight to catch. We have someone who's planning on helping out, but until they arrive, just ask someone here in the hotel to help you. You look like a confused grandpa, so getting assistance shouldn't be a problem."

"He *is* a confused grandpa," Blake mutters under his breath.

I shoot him a look and mouth, *"Not helping."*

Blake blinks slowly, clearly not fussed.

As much as I agree that bringing Kyros with us would be a bad idea, I can't help but feel incredibly responsible for him. I mean, he was brought back from the dead *for me*. So, there's that.

Part of me wishes we could bring him with us, but the other, more intelligent part of me says that's a disaster of epic proportions. Besides, I'm pretty sure Renaldo would kill me.

Kyros stands up, tugging at the tops of his thighs. "How do men in this era handle having their manhood squashed up inside these confines?"

My eyebrows shoot up. "And on that note…" I spin around, zipping up my suitcase, and rolling it over to the door.

"Truly, Anastasios, how do you get used to such restrictions? There's no airflow," Kyros mutters, holding onto the edge of the bed and maneuvering into what I can only conclude was an ostrich impression as he squats up and down.

"It's Blake. And…" Blake's gaze shifts to me then back to Kyros, "you get used to it."

I run my hand over my face. All the marvels this new

age brings and in typical manly fashion, they worry about their bits.

"All right, well, it's time to get going," I say, edging closer to the door, so I can make a quick escape.

"Amarantham," Kyros calls.

I sigh but turn back around. "Yes?"

"It has been an honor to serve you," he says, pulling his shoulders back a bit. He still looks like Gollum, but at least he's got his teeth and modern clothes.

My insides twist and I drop the handle of the suitcase to walk over to him. "It's been an honor to work alongside you, as well. You must know that." I set my hand along his left shoulder, patting it awkwardly.

He steps forward quickly, wrapping his arms around me. With my arms pinned to my sides, I look over my shoulder, trying to plead Blake for help with my eyes. What I get is a half-smirk.

Oh, he'll pay for that.

"Well, I really better..." I begin, trying to free my right hand enough to pat Kyros on the side.

With a sniffle, he releases me and stands up straight. "Well, then, yes. You must be going. I shouldn't keep you."

I stumble backward, trying to gain some clearance. "Take care of yourself." Shooting him a pained smile, I turn around and walk out the open door. I'm on the wraparound outdoor deck before I realize I forgot my suitcase.

"Dammit," I mutter under my breath. Turning back, I stick my arm inside the door, grab the suitcase, and cast another quick wave to Kyros.

Blake's smirk only deepens and I have the sudden urge to hop in the car and drive off without him.

"See ya, old man. Stay out of trouble," Blake says as he closes the door behind us both.

Yeah, like that's gonna happen. He clearly doesn't remember much about Kyros in his past life. He was a hellion then and likely a hellion now.

I make my way to the car and toss the suitcase in the backseat. Everything about this feels surreal and wild. There's practically nothing I can wrap my head around that grounds me.

The ride to the airport is a test in awkward silence. As much as we can be comfortable together without all the mundane chit-chat, I can't bring myself to say anything at all. My mind is numb, almost quiet, and I can tell this is Apollo's way of trying to get me to do his bidding.

He's trying to show me that my gifts are tied to him and that when he pulls back, what's left is simple humanity. But I've got a surprise for him—I wouldn't mind being human for a change. I never wanted this gift or any of the power that rides along with it.

I follow Blake's lead as he maneuvers us through the rental car drop-off and the airport. Thankfully, he's a take-charge kinda guy and there isn't much I need to think about through the whole ordeal. It's not until we're sitting in the airplane that the gravity of my situation slams into me.

"Oh my god, I hate flying," I say, gripping the armrests until my knuckles turn white. My stomach rolls and I'm suddenly not so sure about this whole leaving thing.

"Yeah, you made that abundantly clear last time." Blake

laughs and his lopsided dimple makes an appearance to the side of his goatee. It makes my heart flutter and my insides warm.

If I weren't worried about dropping thousands of feet out of the sky, it would be enough to have me running through scenarios on how to handle our romantic entanglement when we touch down. Gods know Kyros's arrival certainly put the kibosh on any sexiness happening back in Greece and if Ren finds out we're "a thing," but haven't done *the deed...*

I shudder the thought away.

"Oh, right," I say, slinking into my seat a bit. On the way here, I'd basically made a fool of myself. It won't happen again. I need to make a better impression this time.

Besides, the flight attendant is too busy further up. Probably getting ready for this death trap to take off.

"You know, for someone who's lived as long as you have," Blake whispers, with a hint of humor in his tone, "you sure are jumpy about flying."

"Yes, well, now I have you to worry about. Don't I?" I say, shooting him a knowing look. Granted, I'd be a wuss even if he weren't riding with me, but now that I think about it…

"Yeah, but if we were going to crash, you'd have seen it. Right?" he says, leaning in a bit. His eyes sparkle with all seriousness and I swallow hard.

A valid point, but still. My gifts aren't infallible. It's not like I'm a god. I'm just a chick who gets glimpses into the future from time to time.

A strange tingly feeling courses through me, raising

the hair on my scalp and sending goosebumps skittering over my body. My heartbeat kicks up a notch and I'm suddenly concerned about how far Apollo might go to keep me here. He wouldn't bring the plane down knowing I'd survive, but Blake wouldn't. Would he?

Surely I would have gotten a vision if he meant to bring the plane down. Right?

Before I have the chance to do anything about the thought, the pilot announces our departure, and the flight attendant in view buckles herself in.

"Oh god," I mutter under my breath, squeezing my eyes tightly shut.

The plane taxis and the next thing I know, my stomach flips, and we're up in the air.

Blake places his hand over the top of mine, and the warmth from his palm spreads across my skin. I sigh into the comfort, unable to hold my breath any longer.

"We're in the air. You can relax now," he says, nudging me with his shoulder.

"Easy for you to say," I mumble.

After the longest fifteen minutes of my life, the flight attendant makes her way to us. Despite myself, I end up with a stash of teeny tiny bottles of booze. None of them ideal, but they'll do in a pinch.

If I need them.

"Do you want some soda to go along with all that?" Blake asks, grinning wide as he jabs his index finger toward my stash.

I shoot him an irritated glance. "What do you take me for, sir? And, of course. Can I have a 7-up, please?"

The flight attendant nods, handing over a smaller-than-normal can.

I sigh, cracking it open and pouring it into the plastic cup with way too much ice.

"Would you like anything to drink?" the flight attendant says, turning to Blake.

"Whatever cola you have is fine," he says.

She bends down, grabbing the can and shoving a plastic cup into a bucket of ice at the top of her cart. Then she hands them over.

"Thanks," he says, setting them down on the tray in front of him.

She nods and continues on her way.

I take a sip of the 7-up, all the while envisioning cracking open the first bottle of, gods only know what, and downing the contents.

"You don't have to wait, you know," Blake says, tipping his chin toward the bottles.

"No, I'm okay for now," I mutter taking another small sip.

Blake shakes his head, and chuckles under his breath. "So, do you think the old man will be okay?"

Guilt twists me in the gut again and I eye the tiny bottles. "He's a grown man."

"Yeah, but he's pretty green to this new world. Maybe we should have—"

"Do not finish that sentence," I say, pressing my fingertip to his lips, effectively cutting off his words.

"But..." he manages to eke out.

"Shhhhhhh. Trust me. There is no way bringing him with us would have ended well. Besides, can you imagine the brimstone and fire it would invoke with Ren. Oh my god, just...*no*." An involuntary convulsion moves through me. "This is the best way."

I remove my finger from his mouth, dropping my hand beside my cup.

"I suppose you're right. I guess I feel a little guilty about it. He's all alone and even though I don't really remember much about him, per se, I can't help but feel protective over the old man. It's weird," Blake says, turning from me and looking out the window.

"It's probably because you were tasked to protect us both. He was part of my entourage, after all," I say, taking another fizzy sip, wishing I was able to stop thinking about the distance between us and the horizon.

A crackling sensation pierces through at the edge of my mind and I sense him before I see him. The seat in front of us shifts and after much grunting, Kyros's head pops up over top.

"Ah, there you are," he says, grinning broadly. "Well, this is a delight, isn't it?"

Blake turns his wide, brown eyes to me, clearly not used to this real-world full of the supernatural just yet. I, on the other hand, should have known leaving Apollo's request behind wouldn't be so easy.

"Oh, yeah. I'm fucking tickled to death," I mumble, grabbing hold of the first bottle of booze and cracking it open.

4

GET UP AND OWN THE DAMN DAY

I sense the bright light before I gather the energy to open my eyes. It presses on the back of my lids, alerting me to the intense pain in my head ready to greet me the moment I try to sit up.

Groaning, I reach over my head and cover it with my pillow.

Pillow?

Despite myself, I yank it off my head and attempt a mini-cobra.

Or is that Sphinx? Lord help me, I was never any good at yoga.

Light streams into my bedroom and I stare out the window, dumbfounded. How in the hell did I get here? Why do I remember nothing?

Then, snippets of a plane ride filter back in.

Oh, gods...

I plop unceremoniously, face down on the pillow, and groan again.

Beside me, I hear the sound of someone clearing their throat and I scramble to sit up.

In the corner of my room, a pile of clothing on my small wicker chair moves. Kyros attempts to stand, careful to set the clothing back where it originated.

Despite myself, a startled scream escapes my lips.

"What in the hell are you doing in here?" I sputter, clutching my blankets to my chest.

My head throbs, a remnant of my indiscretion on the plane, and likely a side-effect that prevented me from sensing Kyros in the first place.

"Anastasios demanded I keep an eye on you while he attended to someone named Aiden," Kyros says, puffing up his chest indignantly. He looks utterly ridiculous with the gesture, particularly since his t-shirt of choice is two sizes too big, and says, 'with a body like this, who needs hair?'

How on earth he managed to get it, I'll never know.

"Blake, his name is *Blake*," I say, running a hand over my face.

It's too early for this kind of nonsense. I need Excedrin. STAT.

"Yes, well, he will return soon, but since there wasn't a convenient place to sit, I figured this would do," he says, pointing at the clothing stack. "You know, it wouldn't hurt you to attend to your attire. I mean, honestly, who needs so many choices?"

"Kyros," I say, glowering at him. "As much as I adore being berated first thing in the morning—oh, wait. No, I don't. Get out." I raise my arm, pointing toward the door.

He harrumphs but shuffles himself out into the hallway.

"Wait—I have a question," I say, wondering how much of a fool I made of myself.

"How... Did Blake..." I can't seem to find the words to ask what's on my mind.

Kyros raises his chin, watching me struggle from the end of his nose.

"You were incapacitated, if that's what you're asking. Anas—*Blake*—was a gentleman and ensured you were taken care of until resting in here."

"Did he—?" I wet my lower lip. Gods, I need water, too. "Did he stay here? Or?"

"Yes, Amara—*Diana*. But he took up residence on the floor." He points to the edge of the bed and I lean over. There's a small throw blanket and a couch pillow folded neatly beside my nightstand.

My heart flutters and I feel like a complete moron. I should be better at this by now. I'm sure he thinks I'm real smooth. I'll be lucky if he wants anything to do with me after all of this.

"Did I make a complete idiot of myself?" I say, chewing on the side of my cheek.

Kyros's face screws up and he tries to hide something in his expression. If my gifts were working at full-strength, I'd be able to pick up what, but I can't seem to think through the hangover fog, let alone dig into someone else's head.

"Well, I wouldn't say a *complete* idiot, Amarantham," he finally says.

"Oh, gods," I say, wincing. "What did I do? Do I want to know?"

Kyros clasps his hands in front of his small frame and considers. "Well, you did tell him repeatedly how his smile made you... What was the word? *Squirm* with pleasure? You continually tried to coax one out of him, which I have to admit was highly entertaining. And I believe you mentioned several occasions how you'd have his baby if you could do such a thing."

My stomach rolls and I'm not only mortified but about to be sick. "Classy. Oh dear, god. I wasn't sick though, was I?" I fight the urge to hurl and hold my breath, hoping it passes.

"Oh, no. There was no vomit," Kyros says, walking back into the room and patting me on the shoulder.

I sink back into the bed, rolling over, and returning the pillow over the top of my head.

Well, at least there's that.

Kyros pats my back. "There, there. At least he didn't run screaming for the hills. Remember the good old days? You did that a fair few times to the unbelievers. Granted, he did leave bright and early this morning. So perhaps, I'm speaking too soon."

"Kyros, get out," I mutter, my words muffled between the mattress and pillow.

He clears his throat, but his hand is abruptly missing from my back. "I will just—I'll be out there if you need me."

"Phanx," I say, not bothering to annunciate the word.

When I hear the soft click of the door, I close my eyes and sink further into the bed. If I could drop all the way to the seventh circle of hell, I'd do it. Pretty sure it would be less horrific than my current situation.

Get yourself together, Diana. It was one indiscretion and it's not like he doesn't already know you hate flying. On the upside, he's seen my warts—so if he comes back after all that, it was meant to be. Right?

I inhale a noseful of stale laundry detergent and dust, then toss my pillow aside. Wallowing in self-pity is not the way I want to begin this new life with Blake. We've missed so much time together and I don't want to waste another minute of it. I want to dive into his love and bury myself in it until I feel whole again.

"All right, Diana. Get up and own the damn day," I whisper to myself, brushing back a hot pink chunk of hair. I throw back the bedspread and my stomach flutters. Just like last time, Blake must have removed my pants, likely to make sure I was comfortable. My top half is still in clad the way it was, so I know he didn't try to cop a feel while I was passed out.

When I stand up, the world spins a bit with the pain in my head. I push through it, grabbing a new outfit from the stack of clothes Kyros had been hiding under, and make my way to the bathroom.

After downing some headache tablets, and taking the world's longest shower, I walk out of the bathroom feeling a billion times better. The dull ache in the back of my brain is still there, but it's livable. A blessing from supernaturally fast healing.

Now, I just need some food and I might be able to make it go away completely.

When I walk out into the kitchen, Kyros is butted up

to the two-person breakfast bar and Blake is behind the stove. The scent of bacon fills the space and I take up the seat next to Kyros.

"Anas—*Blake* has returned," Kyros announces as if I hadn't sussed that one out on my own.

I opt for nodding as a response, so I can admire Blake's perfect ass in his stylishly ripped-up jeans. Seriously, I could stare at him all day long.

I sigh far too loudly and Kyros shoots me an odd look.

"What?" I mutter, defensively.

Blake turns around, shooting me a full smile. His dimples appear beside his black goatee and my heart constricts in on itself. "Hey, how are you feeling?"

"Like I was run over by a freight train, then drug for a few hundred miles," I say. "But things are looking up."

His smile doesn't fade as he holds my gaze for a moment. "Well, I figured you'd want something in your stomach to help with all that. Pancakes and bacon sound okay?"

"Are you kidding? You could throw toast at me and I'd be in awe," I say before I can filter myself. I'm not used to people doing things for me, but I could get used to it.

Kyros taps my arm. "What exactly are pancakes?"

I chuckle. "It's sort of like a flatbread, but tastes more like heaven."

He gapes at me.

"Just—you'll see," I say, shaking my head, and instantly regretting the movement. Headache's still hiding in there somewhere.

"Well, he won't have to wait long. It's ready," Blake

says, grabbing some plates from my cupboard like he lives here.

I slide off my stool and make my way to the other cupboard. While he dishes up the pancakes and bacon, I pour each of us a glass of orange juice and grab the syrup.

Blake hands out the plates and I hand everyone their silverware. At least Kyros knows what to do with a fork now and no longer stares at it like it's a magic wand or something.

"Thanks, Blake," I say, reaching out and placing my hand on his arm when he sets his plate at the end of the bar, opting to stand next to me.

"Don't worry about it. It's nice to make breakfast for someone who will actually eat it. Aiden doesn't usually get up until midday, so there's no point in trying with that kid," he chuckles.

"Good point," I say, grabbing the syrup and dousing my pancakes in it.

Kyros eyes me suspiciously, but I reach over and do the same to his. "Trust me, you'll love it."

He narrows his gaze, evidently skeptical. However, the moment he puts the pancake bite in his mouth, his skepticism melts away and he goes to town, scarfing down everything in sight.

Blake and I both laugh and return to our meals. After all the alcohol yesterday, my stomach screams for real food to balance my body back out.

I'm halfway through my pancakes when my green corded phone blares to life on the wall beside me, and I practically jump out of my skin. I'm a hundred percent off my psychic game. No wonder I rarely drink during normal circumstances. This sucks.

I wipe my mouth with a napkin and make my way to the phone. After the fourth ring, I pick up.

"Hello?" I say, shooting a sideways glance to the men at the breakfast bar.

"You're home?" Renaldo scoffs. "I thought I was going to leave another message on your insanely archaic machine."

"What do you need, Ren? I'm having breakfast."

"And why am I just *now* hearing of this?" he says, ignoring my comment. "I should have been the first one to know. I mean, my god, do you know what a royal pain in the backside Mrs. Kaminski—"

"Don't get your panties in a bunch. We just got in late last night," I say, trying to head him off before he goes into full-on meltdown.

"Oh," he breathes. "Well, I guess that's not so bad."

"So, what's up?" I repeat, trying to get this ball rolling. I walk over to the bar again and take my seat, letting the spiral cord stretch across the middle of the room.

"Well, other than your assistant needing a generous pay raise and an extra week of vacation…"

I roll my eyes and lock my gaze on Blake when they come to a stop. He grins back.

Kyros shoots me a confused glance, but I swipe my hand in the air between us. I can only deal with one crazy assistant at a time.

"Ren…" I warn.

"Well, I do," he huffs. "But other than *that*, I thought you'd want to know Demetri called looking for you. He sounded kind of upset and I figured I better do my duty to inform you."

I sit up straighter, suddenly more alert. "What did he say?"

"Not much, I mean, that man doesn't say much. Does he? He's basically mono-syllabic. I honestly don't know how you can—"

"Ren—"

"All right, all right. It's less what he said and more what I'm hearing in the underground," Ren says, his words taking on the tone he likes to use when he's spreading the latest gossip.

"Okay," I say, tapping my fork on the edge of my plate as I try not to imagine stabbing him with it.

"Well, he's pretty much gone MIA. His clients are starting to freak because he's not returning calls and of course, who do they turn to? Well, you're not here, so I'm the one being inundated," he says, back to making this all about him. "Diana, something's gotta be done. Like ASAP. Otherwise, you'll be finding yourself a new assistant, because I will have gone certifiable."

My eyes flit to Kyros. Renaldo's choice of words are somewhat ironic. Not that I'm looking to replace his crazy, incessantly late ass—but if I had no choice…

"Okay, Ren. Take a deep breath. I'll be there in ten."

5

GET LUCKY

"**A**re you sure you don't mind?" I say, standing on the front step to my little granny house, suddenly acutely aware of just how much of a spinster I've become over the past few years.

Blake's brown eyes sparkle and a hint of a smile threatens to blossom across the rest of his features. He leans back against the iron railing, crossing his ankles in a gesture so open and easy, it makes my solar plexus flutter, and a deep aching spreads through the rest of me.

"I think I can handle the old man," Blake says, his tone light and bordering on teasing.

"You know what I mean," I say, shooting him a look. "I'm sure it's the last thing you want to be doing right now, but truth be told, I don't want him tagging along with me for this conversation."

He laughs softly. "Afraid of the wrath of Ren?"

I nod. "Something like that. I need to tread lightly with him or there will be a meltdown situation. I can only handle one unhinged assistant at a time."

"Fair enough," he says, reaching a hand out for me.

I accept it, stepping closer to him. He wraps his arms around my torso, sending a wave of heat through any part of me not yet vibrating with anticipation. My breath hitches as I melt into him, and I'm suddenly extremely glad he can't read my mind.

Since my connection opened to him, I've been actively working to dampen my gifts with him, so he has the privacy of his own thoughts. It was hard at first because I desperately want to know what he's thinking and feeling. But I've found I'm almost as addicted to the mystery of not knowing, too.

I rest my head in the crook of his neck, inhaling his natural scent, burning it into my memory. For a brief moment, I'm cocooned in his embrace, the outside world quiet and peaceful in a way I've not felt for eons.

He sighs contently, his hand rubbing circles across my lower back.

"Amara—*Diana*… Shouldn't you be on your way? I'm certain you mentioned something about ten minutes, and while I'm no expert on this modern time, I'm fairly sure you've gone well past that for whomever you're meant to meet," Kyros says through a crack in the front door.

"Thanks, Kyros. I'll keep that in mind," I say, refusing to open my eyes or make a move.

"Honestly, how you've managed to survive without me, I cannot understand. You need someone who can keep you in line and on time," he says, tsking under his breath.

"And on that note," I say, pushing back to a stand.

Blake's eyes open lazily, a lopsided grin on his face. "Old man, you certainly know how to spoil a moment."

Kyros huffs.

"Go inside. I'll be back as soon as I can and we can introduce Kyros to Aiden," I say, running my hand down Blake's arm. The firm muscle of his tricep is enough to plunge my thoughts right back in the gutter.

For the briefest of moments, I can't help but wonder if he's as good in bed as he is at kissing. This version of him certainly has some moves he didn't have before. Whenever we get around to it, I can't help but fantasize about what new tricks he'll have up his sleeves… Or lack of sleeves?

I squeeze his arm lightly.

Mmmm, definitely lack of sleeves.

My face heats and I pull back my hand like I shoved it in a fire.

Blake shoots me a confused look, but I wave it away with an awkward smile, hoping he'll write it off as just a weird quirk. May as well add to the pile of odd, right?

I clear my throat, suddenly self-conscious and off my game. Gods, I feel like a school kid.

"Well, I better…" I say, jabbing my thumb toward the street.

He tips his chin up. "Go, we'll be waiting."

"Mkay. Well, see ya," I say, waving like a dork.

He laughs and shakes his arm, before going back inside.

I turn around, screwing up my face as I walk down the stairs.

Get a grip, Diana. Honestly.

The walk to Inner Sanctum Books and Gifts thankfully helps clear my head. It's amazing how much a little fresh air can reinvigorate a person. Thankfully, the alcohol yesterday hasn't caused any lasting issues. There's just a fuzzy edge in the back of my brain that's barely noticeable. Instead, what's left is the heightened sexual tension coursing through my body.

Ren is right, I do need to get laid.

I shiver rolls through me and I force myself to focus on the task at hand.

Blake's observations about my reason for leaving the two of them behind were spot on. The last thing I need to do right now is give Renaldo an aneurism. I'll have to introduce Kyros to him slowly. In fact, I'm not even sure how the hell I'm going to explain Kyros at all. It's not as if Ren knows who I really am—or what I really can do.

Sure, he knows I have psychic abilities, but he'd flip his ever-loving mind if he knew just how entrenched in the supernatural world I am.

As it is, I'm not sure if he actually believes the magical world exists—despite the obviousness of it in the world around him. He's so focused on himself that he hardly has time to contemplate anyone or anything else.

I snicker at the thought of what a rude awakening it would be for him, albeit, kinda funny.

As I open the gate to the picket fence surrounding the little cottage we use for the shop, I stop dead. A wave of nostalgia and significance pushes against me and I'm reminded of the way I'd felt just before I'd left.

I knew something was amiss then—something big and unrelated to the missing girls. But I had no idea it would be as monumental as it turned out to be. How could I? My mind was *literally blocked* from seeing it.

A smile breaks across my face. Ren partially got his wish. Blake and I definitely have some chemistry, and a bit more than just *history*, to contend with. There's a good chance I'll break my dry spell, as Ren insists I better, and who knows…maybe I'll even be able to open my heart again. That should make him happy—and get him off my back about my bits shriveling up.

With that thought, I throw back my shoulders and walk up the steps to the front door like I own the place —*because I do.* But as I reach for the door handle, it doesn't budge.

"What the—? *Come on, Ren.* You have to be kidding me. It's ten-thirty," I curse, patting my jeans. Of course, I didn't bring my keys with me, since the store should have been open already. *Like, ages ago.* Leave it to that man to have the audacity to call me and not even be at work.

I dig around the front garden, trying to remember which rock is fake. When I don't find it straight away, I close my eyes and just rely on my gifts. Which, to be honest, I should have just done right off the bat. I guess I've gotten so used to pulling them back a bit, I hadn't noticed the tendency has spread.

Key in hand, I unlock the door, then put the key back, just in case something like this happens again. Because with Ren, you know it will.

As the door creaks open, I'm barraged with the

familiar aroma of Inner Sanctum. It's a heady mixture of incense, tinctures, and essential oils…combined with the smell of used and new books. Gone are all of the Valentine's Day items, and up are a menagerie of gnomes with green top hats (because they in no way look like leprechauns), all holding four-leaf clovers or gold-filled pots. Golden coins, beads, and more clovers can be found in various nooks and crannies.

He's evidently gone a bit bonkers when left to his own devices.

Well, *more* bonkers.

By the desk, a battle has been waged between gnomes and bunnies, as the Ostara decorations and symbols litter the area. Evidently, my assistant wanted both to be represented, but with the sheer amount of green in this room, it's clear he's opted for luck. It's probably a not-so-subtle hint to me that I should get 'lucky' soon. That would be his style, for sure.

I snort, stopping for a moment to take in the room. At least he's kept the storefront up. It looks nice and it's obvious a lot of merchandise has been moved.

However, as expected, Ren is nowhere to be found. Because, when is that guy ever on time?

I roll my eyes, flip on the lights to the store, and make my way to the back room where I typically do my readings. I half expect to find him at my desk, attempting to take over the joint or running a back-room gambling ring. But when I walk in, the place is exactly as I left it. Barely an item touched.

I'm going to have to call him.

Without turning the lights on, I walk over to the reading table. I trail my fingertips along the glass as I take in all of the items and do a mental inventory. Tarot cards, crystals, favorite candles, spare shoes. Everything of importance is here and accounted for.

I can tell I haven't been onsite to do readings, though. The energy of the space is muted—almost empty of the power it usually exudes. Plus, there's no line or random person waiting to pounce on me the moment I get in. For a while, that was the norm, rather than the exception to the rule. It's kinda nice to come in unnoticed for a change.

I walk from the reading table to my desk on the other side of the room. The large mahogany desk is the one splurge I wanted in the space and it's traveled with me over the years because it has a presence all its own. It's for those times when I found myself alone and needed guidance and strength. Over the years, I've leaned on its energetic properties. There've even been times when I've hidden myself away in the footwell and allowed it to hide me when I was done dealing.

Flipping through the stack of mail on my desk, I toss the junk mail in the bin and shuffle the bills to the middle, so I can deal with those later. Obviously, Ren wasn't super interested in the business side of the business. He's more interested in spending money than paying for the necessities.

Sighing to myself, I reach for the phone, but as I start to dial, something stops me. I can't put my finger on what it is exactly, but something feels slightly off. Before I have a chance to do a proper psychic assessment, the door behind me clicks open, and a figure races at me with something in hand.

I have just enough time to process the situation as a metallic garden rake swings at my head.

6

ASSISTANT DIVAS

"*R*enaldo, what in the actual hell are you doing?" I blurt out, ducking as the metal rake embeds itself into the wall behind me. It knocks off a set of ceramic angels older than he is by a couple of centuries and dislocates a large painting given to me by Salvador Dali.

Not that Ren would know any of that.

His eyes are wide and wild, but as soon as realization slaps him upside his thick head, he lets go of the handle of the rake, and it drops unceremoniously to the floor with a loud thunk. Covering his mouth with splayed fingers, he unleashes a squeal that would rival a little kid in a haunted house.

"Oh my god, Diana. I didn't know it was you," he squeaks.

My eyebrows push down and I stare at him. "I *told* you I was coming. Who else do you think it would be?"

He grins at me sheepishly. "Well, I thought you were kidding. Like, maybe it was a metaphor for…"

I quirk an eyebrow.

"Okay, look…" he says, dropping his hands to place one over his heart and one on his hip. "I lost track of time and then I started questioning if I remembered you saying what you said. It's been an absolute cluster over here, Diana. You have *no* idea. I swear, my mind is a scrambled mess. I don't know how you do it. I really don't," Renaldo rambles, running a hand through his hair. Ordinarily, his dark locks would be meticulously groomed, side part expertly crafted, but right now, it's all stood on end, like he'd had a fight with a light socket and lost.

When he said he was going nuts, it's pretty clear the crazy train left the station a while ago.

I slow blink at him, trying hard to summon the strength not to burst out laughing.

He bends down, picking up the rake, and setting it against the wall. Turning back to me, he tries again to smooth out the wild strands. Anxiety, fear, and something else surrounds him in such thick bands, it's hard to tell what's the biggest cause.

"Ren, sit and take a breath. I need to know what's going on," I say, pointing to the reading table.

His eyes follow the trail my fingertip dictates, and his head bobs up and down in acceptance. He practically shuffles to the seat usually meant for clients, then slumps into it. I take up my seat, clasping my hands together and placing them on the glass table between us.

Seeing him so rattled, I can't help but wish I had the special ability to calm people down or heal their emotions. It certainly would come in handy now.

After a few moments of slow, deliberate breaths, he

glances up.

"What's really going on, Ren? I can't get a read on you, your emotions and thoughts are all over the place," I say quietly.

Typically, I make it a point not to pry into the lives of people I know and love unless absolutely necessary, but this is a special circumstance. When people are hysterical, sometimes things come to me faster and with more clarity. However, it's not the case now and it's actually giving *me* anxiety in trying.

After another slow inhalation, he whispers, "I'm just so...*relieved*."

"That's not what it feels like," I say, still trying to make sense of his conflicting emotions.

"Ever since you left, things have steadily gotten crazier. I mean, at first, it was normal crazy. Mrs. Kaminski—well, you know," he says, some of his usual humor glinting in his eyes. "But then, with Demetri down for the count, it was like the floodgates of hell opened up and wanted to swallow me whole. I've been fielding calls practically nonstop from people trying to get in to see you. Then, when I told them you were gone..." he shudders, "some of them resorted to storming in, just to be sure. They thought I was keeping you captive or something. Can you believe that?" He snickers, bracing his fingertips against his chest.

The knowing comes to me quickly. *He'll be okay once things settle.*

"You have no idea how glad I am you're really, truly here," he continues.

My lashes flutter across my cheeks and I focus on the

sensation as a way to ground me to this news. Guilt wells up inside me. Leaving when I did practically pushed Ren into a full-on nervous breakdown, that much is evident. I rake my fingertips across my forehead, trying to process.

"Okay, well, first things first, I need to know about Demetri. Then, we'll deal with the client situation next," I say, locking my gaze to his.

Renaldo's nostrils flare, but he nods.

"So, Demetri isn't returning calls from his clients and has gone MIA. When did he call you?" I ask.

"Last night. But Diana, I should also mention…when he did speak…he didn't sound right," he says, deep wrinkles carving through the space between his eyebrows.

If Ren's worried about him, something must be going on.

"How so?"

He considers for a moment, his eyes darting back and forth in his recollection. I tap into his thoughts and concern blossoms like a bursting star in the center of my torso.

"It felt like…" Ren trails off, but his thoughts come in loud and clear now.

"Like he was trying to say goodbye?" I whisper, horrified.

Ren makes a face, but nods. "That's what I'm afraid of."

"Shit," I curse. I knew losing his gifts would hurt Demetri, but I didn't realize how fragile that connection was. How tied to his identity they were. Okay, so I'm gonna need to make a trip. He can be stubborn when he wants to be and I have to get a read on him in person."

Again, Ren nods. "What do you want me to do about the crazies who keep calling? They aren't going to be placated much longer, Diana."

I open my mouth, but the words get stolen before they can escape.

"Allow me to handle them," Kyros says, suddenly standing in the doorway.

My mouth pops open and Ren spins around on his seat like he's ready to reach for the rake.

Seconds later, Blake bursts into the store and then to the doorway. "Goddammit, old man. You can't up and vanish like that," he says, grabbing hold of Kyros by the upper arm. He tries to pull him back, but Kyros doesn't budge.

Renaldo's eyes widen, as he glances from Kyros to me, then back again. For once, he's speechless, but I'm not certain that's a good thing.

Over the past week, Kyros's capacity for speaking English has grown to the point where he barely speaks in Ancient Greek anymore. Clearly, a byproduct of his magical resurrection. And likely so he can help me better.

Thanks, Apollo.

"Who is this guy?" Ren scoffs, standing up and striking his best diva pose.

Blake shoots me a look of apology, doubling over as he tries to catch his breath. "Sorry, Diana. He up and vanished. Somehow I knew he'd be here."

"Would one of you bitches tell me what's going on here?" Ren says, clearly not amused. "Are you trying to...*replace me?*"

I stand as well, bracing my hands out in front of me. "No, Ren. It's nothing like that."

"And who exactly is this?" Kyros asks, puffing up his chest and hobbling into the room.

He's still wearing the ridiculous t-shirt. If anything he looks more like an escaped nursing home patient than someone to replace Ren with. Then again, Ren's not far off from the truth of being replaced. At least, if Kyros has anything to say about it.

This is not going to go well.

"Who am I?" Ren says, a nervous laugh bubbling from his lips as he widens his stance, his hands flailing about. "*I'm* Diana's right hand and manage all of her affairs. Just who the hell are you?"

Irritation radiates off him and without a doubt, I know he's not wrong. My mouth snaps shut.

"Why do you allow such insolence, Amar—*Diana*?" Kyros says, a flare of protectiveness rolling off of him in waves. He rounds on Ren. "Do you know who you're speaking to?"

"Kyros, stop. It's okay. Renaldo's right, this is a discussion best left for another day," I say, switching my gaze from Kyros to Blake. I try to will him the thought to get Kyros out of here from a single glance. Luckily, he gets the point.

"Come on, Kyros. Let Diana do her thing. She's got this," Blake says, urging Kyros to exit the reading room.

Kyros doesn't budge. His eyes narrow as they flit between me and Ren.

"Kyros, go with Blake. Please," I say, reiterating the

sentiment. "This will all get sorted. We'll talk when I get home. Okay?"

His expression flattens and I can tell he's ready to rebuff. So, for the first time since we got back to Helena, I use the psychic connection between us.

Kyros, don't argue with me. Ren doesn't know anything about me. He'll need to be brought around slowly.

Kyros swallows down whatever rebuttal he had in mind, and nods curtly, thank the gods. Without another word, he manages to make turning around the most arduous of tasks. Then he shuffles out of the room, taking the lead in front of Blake, who shrugs at me.

"See you in a bit?" Blake asks, shooting an anxious gaze toward the backside of a retreating Kyros.

"Yeah, I won't be long," I say, scrunching my face and casting a sideways grin. There's so much I wish I could tell him. Like it won't always be this weird. But I shouldn't make any promises I can't keep.

"Okay," he says, nodding. For a moment he hovers in between the doorways, then waves awkwardly before chasing after Kyros.

I bite my lip, sighing to myself as I take in the backside of him as he leaves. After a moment, I glance over and catch Ren's eyebrow quirk up, his romance radar going off.

Holding out a hand, I try to stop him before he starts. "I'll tell you all about it later."

"Oooh, so there's something to know?" he says, his voice bordering on scandalized.

I shake my head. "Demetri is the priority here, remember?"

Ren scrunches up his face, clearly fighting internally. "I s'pose."

Walking over to my desk, I reach for the receiver on the large, bordering on archaic desk phone. I'm not entirely sure how old it is, but it's been in my possession since the fifties. Just as I'm about to call Demetri to see if I can pop in for a visit, the phone rings. For the briefest of moments, I figured it was Demetri and his unique ability to always sense when I was going to call him. Then I remembered his gifts are gone.

I shoot a look to Ren, who widens his eyes in an evident question of whether or not I'm going to get it. Clearly, he's no longer fussed by the phone ringing since I'm here to answer it instead of him.

I pick up the receiver. "Hello?"

"Diana? Glad I caught you. It's me, Dan. Got a second?" the detective's voice echoes from the other end.

I'm barely back a day and it's as if the whole world got the memo.

Dropping into the leather-bound desk chair, I run my hand through my pink hair. There's so much to do, but if there's one person besides Demetri I wouldn't want to blow off, it's him. "Sure, Dan. What's up?"

"Well, I have a case here and I don't know how to make heads or tails of it. But I think it might just be in your wheelhouse. Any chance you have a spare minute to help out? I don't think it'll take long."

I run my hand over my face and sigh. If it's not one thing, it's another.

So much for getting back home quickly.

"Of course, what do you need?"

7

TRUST IS MORE THAN SKIN-DEEP

ifteen minutes later, Detective Dan Radovich is sitting across from me at my glass reading table. His dark blue eyes betray the questions hiding in the crevasses of his mind. He's dying to know more about the trip to Greece, but he feels it's not his place to ask.

He and I never had a very personal relationship, but he respects our work friendship more than most. I've always liked that about him. In some ways, he's the only reason I've bothered helping with cases coming out of the Helena PD. He's open-minded enough to deal with me, for starters.

Renaldo has vanished into the main shop, doing whatever it is he does to make the storefront presentable. He's even humming to himself, which I take as a good sign since I don't have the bandwidth to check in on his mental health right now. Ya gotta hand it to him, the man can compartmentalize with the best of them.

Dan crosses his left foot over the top of his right knee

and leans back. In the fluidity of the gesture, he slides a manila folder across the open space of the table.

Before I even touch it, I get glimpses of a young boy, fifteen or sixteen years old at a push. His broad smile is infectious, but his physical appearance, including his beautiful brown skin and messy black hair, instantly take backstage to the deep intelligence pulsing through his aura. He's profoundly gifted, that much is for sure. Yet, this entire power package is wrapped up in a disabled body, as my awareness zones in on the wheelchair that has become a permanent extension of him.

My heart constricts at the injustice of someone so young being dealt such a hand in life. I place my palm on the packet and glance up at Dan, waiting for his assessment first.

"This *should* be a straightforward case," he begins. "Hell, the captain thinks so—but I'm not so sure." Dan shakes his head, his eyes going distant. "Something feels...*off.*"

Opposing emotions well up inside him, pointing toward a deep conviction to protect the young man. However, the full reasoning is still fuzzy in my perception.

"Tell me what's happening," I say, tapping into the visuals and memories as he recalls them.

"Well, you'll get a feel for the case when you look at the file, but the gist is—there's a fourteen-year-old boy who's been getting harassed, for lack of a better word. It seems like it started casually. The family noticed a vehicle following them. At first, they thought nothing of it.

Figured it was just someone who lived in the area who was on the same schedule."

I get flashes of a black SUV with deeply tinted windows. There's an edge of something magical surrounding its encasement—like they can mask themselves or ward off those with special abilities.

I sit up a bit straighter, my curiosity certainly piqued.

"However," he continues, "things have progressed and the parents are getting worried about their son. Now, someone's been hacking into his tech—computers, cellphone. Messages are popping up, trying to pry information out of Jonas—that's the kid. That's when his parents came to us. At first, we all thought he managed to get himself on a site he shouldn't have. The kid's smart, without a doubt. But we found no evidence of that."

"What about the messages? What's happening there?" I ask.

Dan's forehead furrows. "On one hand, they seem cryptic. Stuff like, *'We know what you can do.'* And, *'We're the only ones who can keep you safe.'* When we asked Jonas about it, he seems as confused as the rest of us." He taps the edge of the glass with the tip of his index finger. "But the more I think about it, the more I gotta wonder if there's something special to this kid, if you know what I mean. I was hoping…"

"You were hoping I'd be able to get a read on him," I say, finishing his thought. "Let you know if he has powers of some sort."

Dan's lips press tight and he nods curtly.

For the first time, I flip open the packet on the table. "Well, he does." I stare at the photograph paper-clipped to the upper right-hand corner of the first page. The photo is at least a year or two old, based off of the vision of him I was getting, but one thing that hasn't changed—his smile is infectious.

"Knew it," he mutters under his breath.

I continue to scan the pages, allowing my gaze to flow toward the most important components of the report.

Jonas Fletcher, fourteen-years-old. Born April 12th. Incredibly gifted student. Well-liked at school. Born with transverse myelitis. Permanently disabled and wheel-chair-bound.

"So, what do I do, Diana? How do I let the family know I'm sympathetic? I'm sure they don't want to tell me the whole truth. Why would they? White cop, black family. The stereotypes are all stacked up against them," he says, a bit of agitation bleeding through his demeanor. "Add the supernatural stuff on top…" He shakes his head.

Dan's a good cop and cares deeply about doing the right thing. But he knows all too well how things could go sideways, even with the best intentions. While the world is starting to accept the supernatural world, there are still those who can't—no, *won't*—believe. Plus, all of the human biases are active and in play.

A hint of a smile makes its way to my lips. "Honestly, I think there's only one way to handle this one. You'll have to get them here or bring me along for a chat."

"And you think that will help them to trust me?" he asks, narrowing his gaze. "No offense, Diana, you're as white as I am. Maybe they'd be better off with someone like Martinez."

I shake my head. "Trust is more than skin-deep, Dan.

You know that. Besides, you're the best detective on the force. We can show the Fletchers what else is possible. I'll show them what I can do. Then, if push comes to shove, trust won't matter as much, since I'll be able to get a better read on Jonas. Right now, I can tell he's gifted, I just can't explain how. Or what the nature of his power is. I need to strengthen the connection to him," I say, closing the folder and sliding it back to him.

"All right. Let me see what kind of arrangements I can make. I'll get back to you with some times," Dan says, his eyelashes fluttering with his rapid thoughts. He wants desperately to get this sorted out so he can continue with his investigation, but there's a deep knowing that he can't push this step or it could blow up in his face. And mine too, since he brought me into the mix.

"Sounds good," I say, as I stand up. "And don't worry, Dan. It will all work out. I have a good feeling about that much."

He hefts out a relieved sigh. "I sure as hell hope so. Jonas is a good kid. I don't know what he's gotten mixed up in, but I'll be damned if I'm gonna let anything bad happen to him on my watch."

"Then he's incredibly lucky," I say, shooting him a determined look, hoping it presses home the point.

With a sniff, he tips his head and heads for the door. "Thanks, Diana. I'll be in touch."

Without another word, he makes his way through the store.

One problem potentially on the way to resolution. *Now, about Demetri...*

Dan says his goodbye to Renaldo, who's instantly in

the doorway, not giving me time to even make it to the phone. His eyes sparkle with curiosity, clearly dying to get a read on the latest gossip.

I raise an eyebrow and smirk at him.

After a moment, he heaves a heavy sigh and raises his hands in mock prayer. "Diana, lovely boss of mine, you're killing me here." He enters the room, still praying to some god or another.

"Renaldo, ever-late assistant of mine, it's an open case," I say, drawing out his impatience. "I shouldn't be discussing it until there's a resolution. Maybe not even then."

"Oh, puleeze," he breathes. "As if I'd have anyone to even blab to. You need someone to confide in, and as always, I am willing to pull up my big boy britches to carry that burden." He flutters his eyelashes and puts on his best impression of a sweet smile.

"Oh, yes. Ever the sword-falling type." I chuckle.

"Diana," he whines, dropping his hands to his side and tipping his chin upward like a petulant child. "You have no idea how boring it's been around here. Throw me a bone, please."

"Boring? I thought you said it was *so stressful*?" I say the last two words complete with air quotes. Toying with him like this always brings a smile to my face, and I can tell he's grateful for the normalcy it brings, despite his frustration.

He glares at me.

"Look, there's not much to tell yet, but as soon as I know more, you'll be the first to know," I say, walking to my desk so I can return to the phone call to Demetri that got interrupted.

His face scrunches and he crosses his arms. "Then, do you wanna at least tell me about the grumpy old man, so I don't take every mental highway to anxietyville?"

"I thought you didn't want to know?" I mutter, glancing at the phone, then the clock.

It's been two hours since I left the house. Hopefully, Blake can keep Kyros under control just a little longer. I've never had kids, but from what I can tell, dealing with him is like having a toddler to keep track of. I can only imagine how bizarre this is, since we've barely become a couple.

Nothing like jumping straight into the fire.

I scratch at the side of my forehead, realizing it's probably better to deal with this now.

"Okay, what do you want to know?" I ask, treading the waters lightly. Reaching out with my abilities, I try to assess what information he's looking for, so I can give him just enough to put him at ease.

He places a hand on his hip and flicks the other wrist up in the air. "Well, for starters, what did he mean by '*Do you know who you're speaking to?*'" Ren says, catching me slightly off guard. I figured he'd be more concerned about the dynamic he's playing in terms of "team Diana."

I chew on the side of my lip, putting my feelers out.

"Oh, no…don't you be doing that. I know that look. No using your psychicness to psych me out. Just answer the question," he says, lowering his eyebrows. "After the past few weeks of craziness, you owe me that much."

He's right. Ren's been with me for a number of years

now and he's always been a faithful friend. He could have asked me any number of times why I don't seem to age, but he never has—and I doubt even he's that self-centered not to notice.

On the other hand, I'm acutely aware of what he's capable of dealing with, and the full scope of things might not be it. Hell, I'm not even sure I can deal with it right now.

I glance longingly at the phone, sigh, and walk back to the reading table. I press my hands to the back of my chair and lean forward, deliberating.

"All right. But I think you'll want to sit down for this…" I begin.

8

LOST CAUSES

*R*enaldo quirks an eyebrow and crosses his arms. "He's your *grandpa*?"

I plaster on a sympathetic smile and nod.

Ren's BS-o-meter is probably picking up what I'm laying down, but the excuse is believable enough that he's struggling to fully question it.

I gotta hand it to him, he's more intuitive than I give him credit for.

"Then why did you call him Kyros instead of gramps or something?" he asks, his expression hardening.

"He gets confused. Part of the dementia. We use his name to keep him grounded to reality," I say, surprised at how easily the lies come.

If I weren't immortal, I'd be heading straight to hell, or Tartarus, or the underworld—whatever you want to call it these days. However, I trust my instincts and I know without a doubt that Renaldo would lose his ever-loving mind if he knew the whole truth. If I can protect him from all of this craziness, I'm going to. Or at least do my damnedest.

He mulls over my words, narrowing his eyes, as he untangles his arms and presses his palms over his knees. "Well, I guess that does explain a few things," he says, exhaling deeply. "At least that means I don't have to worry about working with him. My *god*, could you imagine?" His eyes nearly bug out of his head and he fans himself like the thought alone might make him faint.

I chuckle. "Funnily enough, I can."

He shudders in response.

"Oh, behave. He's not that bad," I say, trying hard not to smirk.

The truth is, Kyros and Renaldo have a lot of tendencies in common. They're both fiercely loyal, great with the clientele, and gay. Granted, I'm pretty sure that last tidbit would throw Ren over the edge.

However, as I consider the similarities, my connection to Ren makes more sense than it ever has.

Could it be that a part of me remembered working with Kyros, even though my memory of being the Oracle was locked? Or at least the *idea* of him?

"What?" Ren says, suddenly self-conscious under my scrutiny. He pinches a strand of his hair as if he might find something stuck in it.

"Nothing," I say, shaking my head. "I'm just happy to be back. I missed your crazy ass."

His features soften, as I knew they would. He can't resist a compliment. Backhanded or otherwise. A slow grin spreads across his lips.

"All right, before you get too big of a head, can I make

that call to Demetri?" I ask, tilting my head toward my desk.

Ren sits up a little straighter, his head bobbling on his neck slightly as he weighs his additional questions against his own worry for Demetri. I sit back and wait, feeling the tide in his emotions turn back again toward helping Demetri.

"Yeah, you better get on that. I know I'd feel a lot better knowing you were able to talk some sense into that man," Ren says, his voice betraying the fact that he does actually care about others more than he lets on.

I smile at him and nod. "Good."

He gets up, then walks over to the doorway leading to the front of the store. He stops in the archway and turns back. "Just so you know, I'll hold clients off for as long as I can, but I make no promises as to how long that will be."

"Thanks, Ren," I say, understanding full well he means for today. No one knows I'm back yet, so if I want to have some time to myself, I'll need to grab it now.

His lips press into a thin line. "It's what I do." He runs his hand through his hair and straightens his shoulders with cocky flair. With head held high, he does a mock hair toss and stalks off.

I huff a quiet laugh and walk to the phone. Without a second thought, I dial Demetri's number.

Practically holding my breath, I listen to the ring of the phone until the machine picks up.

"Hey, this is Demetri Lykaios but looks like you missed me. Drop me a message and I'll get back to you."

BEEP.

"Hi Demetri, it's Diana. Renaldo said you called. If

you're there, pick up," I say, closing my eyes and putting my feelers out into the universe. Part of me anticipates the crackle of the phone as it disconnects the machine. When it doesn't happen, I pinch the bridge of my nose, trying to force my mind to locate him.

Instead of getting a pulse on where Demetri is, an uneasy feeling settles in the pit of my stomach and I clench my jaw.

"Demetri? Are you there?" I repeat, panic seeping into my voice. "All right, don't answer. I'm on my way."

I hang up the phone, knowing full-well this means even more time away from Blake and Kyros, but it's unavoidable. If something is wrong with Demetri and I did nothing to check it out, I wouldn't be able to live with myself.

Picking up the phone, I call my home number. Blake answers on the third ring.

"Hey, Blake, it's me," I say, sighing as I slump into my leather chair.

"Uh-oh. That doesn't sound good," he says.

"I'm really sorry. I know I said I wouldn't be gone long, but I need to check in on Demetri," I say, unsure just how much detail I should go into. He already knows about the call, since I filled him in quick before I left, but there's a strange edge of anxiety talking to Blake about Demetri. I suppose it's thanks to the fact that Demetri and I had a passing fling before we realized it wasn't going to work.

"Everything okay?" he asks.

"I'm not sure. I haven't been able to get ahold of him and after talking to Ren, I'm worried. I just want to check in on him quick to make sure he's all right," I say, tapping the desk beside the phone. "Will you be okay for a little longer?"

There's a bit of a pause, but he says, "I think we can manage."

"Thanks, Blake. Really, I'm so sorry. I'll be back as soon as I can and I promise, I'll make it up to you," I say, ignoring the guilt riding me in waves.

"I like the sound of that," Blake teases. I can hear the smile in his voice and a shiver rolls through me as the implications weave through my mind.

Without meaning to, I whimper a little too loudly.

Blake chuckles. "Go, Diana. Do what you need to do. But hurry back, if you can. I'm making arrangements, so we can go to dinner. *Without* Kyros."

"You are?" I say, my pulse quickening with the idea. It's not often I'm caught unaware, but when I am it seems to be with him. I kinda like it.

"Just be back here by six, okay?" Blake says, his voice almost husky.

My eyes flick to the clock. "It's barely gone noon."

"Then you should have no trouble," he practically purrs. "Talk to you soon, beautiful."

He hangs up without giving me a chance to say goodbye.

I set the receiver down and moan softly.

A dinner with Blake sounds heavenly. If I can just get to that point...

"All right, Diana, let's knock some sense into Demetri, so I can get back and enjoy the rest of the day," I whisper to myself, as I make a quick escape through the back garden.

Demetri's house isn't far if you're in a car, but when you're walking it still takes a good half hour. Thankfully the spring day has warmed enough that the walk there is enjoyable.

By the time I'm standing on his front stoop, I've thoroughly fantasized about the way my dinner date with Blake might turn out. As much as I would love to sneak into his mind and get an idea of what he's up to, I continually remind myself that being surprised is a thing of beauty.

Now, however, reality is slapping me upside the head and I know this conversation with Demetri will likely be a buzzkill, regardless of how necessary it might be.

Demetri and I have always had a fairly easy-going relationship, even after the romance fizzled. But now, I just feel awkward as I raise my hand to knock on the door.

"You're a big girl, just get this over with," I mutter under my breath. Without allowing myself a chance to change my mind, I rap my knuckles against the wood as hard as I can.

I take a step back, waiting. In the past, Demetri's powers would have alerted him to my presence, and he would have been inside the door, ready to invite me in. This time, the silence that expands between my knock grows with my anxiety.

Taking a step toward the door, I knock again. "Demetri? It's Diana," I call out, hoping hearing my voice will be enough to get him to come to the door.

I close my eyes, allowing my mind to settle and my gifts to take over. The knowing pulses through my being.

He's inside. That much is certain. The rest is a big question mark.

A fresh wave of anxiety blooms inside my gut and I slam the side of my hand against the door.

"Demetri," I say again, louder this time, "come to the goddamn door, or I swear to all that's holy, I will make a spectacle out here. I know you're in there."

I don't exactly know what kind of spectacle, but I'm sure I'll think of *something*.

Luckily, I don't have to consider the possibilities too long because the lock behind the door clicks back and opens a crack.

"What do you want?" Demetri asks, his voice gruff and his words slightly slurred.

"Have you been drinking?" I blurt out.

"What's it to you? You the alcohol police now, too?" Demetri snorts.

My mouth snaps shut. "You know what I mean. God, Demetri, it's barely gone noon."

His gray-blue eyes are watery and he blinks slowly at the comment. However, he doesn't say a thing.

Sighing to myself, I take a step back. "Look, Ren's worried about you and now so am I."

"Well, yippie," he mutters. "I now rank *'worry'* by the great and powerful Diana Hawthorne."

"Oh, stop. What the fuck is this, Dem? This isn't like you—"

"Like me?" he growls, opening the door wider. The stench of alcohol and body sweat rolls out and I do my best not to wrinkle my nose. "Nothing's like me anymore.

Not even me. So, what difference does any of it make? Maybe this is the *new* me."

"So, you're...*what?* Gonna throw in the towel? What the hell kind of mentality is that?" I spit. "Maybe the universe was right in taking away your abilities if this is how you treat your life—like it doesn't matter at all."

"The universe didn't take away my gifts, Diana. *You did*," he fires back. "Your obsession with your damn past finally backfired big-time. Only, I'm the one who paid the price."

I open my mouth to tell him how it didn't backfire. That I remember everything now thanks to his sacrifice, but I think better of it. Instead, I glare at him and clench my fists.

He tips his chin and smiles sardonically. "Yeah, that's what I thought. You know damn well this reverb should have been yours."

"Maybe it should have," I say, my voice barely a whisper. "That's why I'm here. I want to help. We can figure this out and fix it."

Demetri huffs out a laugh. "Wow, your delusion of grandeur knows no bounds, does it? You walk around like you're a god, Diana. But I have a news flash for you— you're not. This is out of your control. Thanks for your offer, but I think I'll pass. You've done enough damage."

"Demetri—" I say, taking a step toward him.

"Go away, Diana. Ignore what I said to Renaldo. I was drunk and said some shit. I'm a lost cause, but I'll figure it out on my own. Cut me loose and be a big deal somewhere else," Demetri says, slamming the door in my face.

Part of me wants to kick the door down so I can talk

some sense into him. But the wiser part of me—the more knowing part—tells me I need to let him sit in his misery for now. It's enough for him to know I came to talk to him. That I made the effort. Even if he wants to shut me out at the moment.

But if he thinks this is over, he's far off base. I'll be back and I will get through to him—or help him somehow. He's right about all of this being my fault.

Now, it's up to me to fix it, even if he doesn't think it's possible.

God, I am not, but I do know a few, dammit. And they're gonna help if I have anything to say about it.

WHAT IN GOD'S NAME?

*H*ow did I get myself into such a big mess?

On one hand, my life has never felt more complete. My memories continue to fill in gaps that have been missing for as long as I can remember. In addition, the draw to Blake is so intense at times, I can hardly imagine my life before I realized who he was and how important he is to me.

But there are still so many pieces of my past that have cracked wide open and I need to fix them before they blow up in my face.

I take a deep breath, allowing the warm spring air to calm my nerves as I walk.

I'd love nothing more than to go home, wrap myself in Blake's arms and forget any of these problems exist. But I know myself better than that. Without a resolution, I'm going to be a ball of nervous energy and suffice it to say, that's not great date material.

How am I going to be able to enjoy dinner with Blake knowing Demetri is teetering on the edge? My only consolation is that if Demetri did try something crazy—I'm ninety-eight percent sure I'd get a heads up from my gifts. He's been too much a part of my life these past few years.

Houses fly by in my periphery, as I lose myself in my thoughts. Both my mind and my psychic abilities get to work, as I try to find a solution to the problem. Unfortunately, outcomes shift through my mind like sand, with no clear guidance rising to the surface.

Without meaning to, I find myself at the backside of Inner Sanctum, my feet instinctively carrying me to the most prominent place in my world. At least, it was.

For a moment, I internally debate whether or not I should keep walking or head inside. But something niggles at the back of my awareness, like I *should* be here. Perhaps it's so I can unwind a bit before heading out on my date? If anyone can help me get in the right mindset, it's Ren.

Smirking to myself, I take step toward the back gate and unlatch the lock to enter the garden. The moment I swing the gate open, Renaldo spins around with a high-pitched yelp that could rival a little girl's.

His splayed hands fly to his mouth, and his dark eyes are tiny dots in a sea of white. After a second, he fans himself with one hand to evidently keep from fainting. "Diana-*bloody*-Hawthorne, don't *do* that."

I narrow my gaze and speak slowly, suddenly suspicious. "Don't enter my place of work?"

"You know what I mean, for crying out loud," he sputters, opting to drop his splayed fingertips to his chest.

"I really don't," I say, blinking slowly.

He gapes at me. "For someone so psychic, you sure are dense." Twisting around, he stands on his tip-toes and peers into the windows of my reading room.

"What are you doing?"

"What does it look like? I'm *hiding*," Ren says, clutching the collar of his shirt like it's a cloak of invisibility.

I open myself to the energies in and around the store, but I don't find anything out of place.

"I'm not sensing—"

"Shhhhh—" Renaldo says, cutting me off. He ducks and gropes for me on the way down.

I crouch down with him, unable to stop the giggles from erupting. "Are you hiding from Brody?"

He shoots me a confused look. "What? No—I'm hiding from the giganta-line of people who want to have a word with, and I quote, *'the most powerful psychic in the world.'*" He ends the sentence complete with air quotes.

"What?" I stand up, trying to peer through the windows the way Renaldo had.

He grabs hold of my hand and tugs me back down. "Are you insane? They'll see you—"

"But shouldn't you be dealing with them? Get them on the books?" I say, trying to be reasonable as I fight off the internal alarms sounding in the back of my mind.

Why can't I sense them? And how the hell did they know I was back?

Most. Powerful. Psychic.

"Shit," I sputter, running my hand over my face.

Ren shoots me an annoyed look. "What in god's name now?"

God's name is about right.

"Shit, shit, shit," I repeat, as I pace the central walkway in the back garden.

I knew leaving Greece wasn't going to be the end of things. Apollo's been hiding his intentions from me, pulling back my abilities just enough so I didn't question it.

"Dammit," I spit. "Okay, look, Ren...we need to deal with them. They're not going to go away."

"Have you lost your mind? The line practically goes around the block," he squeaks.

I straighten my shoulders, settling into the resolve I feel growing. If Apollo thinks he's going scare me back to Greece by invoking everyone here with a pressing question, he's got another think coming. In ancient times, I could see thousands of people a day without batting an eye.

"We can handle this," I say, reaching for the door.

"Like hell, we can," he says, his hands swinging out in diva style. "No offense, but have you met you? You barely let me put five people a day on your books and you want to deal with a *horde*? Kid you not, it's a horde. Did you hit your head on the way to Demetri's?"

I close my eyes and inhale sharply through my nose.

Shit, he's right.

"Well, what do you propose we do? Hide in the garden for the rest of the day? I have a date with Blake tonight and I'll be damned if I miss it," I mutter, dropping my hand from the door and taking a step back.

For the briefest of moments, Renaldo looks like he's about to get excited over the prospect of my date—but the back gate that I came through rattles. Without missing a beat, he races past me and clicks the lock into place.

"I heard that. I know you're back there—" someone says from the other side. The gate rattles again, pulsing in and out, like they're trying to yank it open despite the enormous steel lock.

Renaldo rushes back to me, grabbing hold of my arm, as he hides behind me. He pushes me forward a bit like I'm the sacrificial lamb. "See what I mean? They're ca-razy," he hisses. "Oh my god, we're going to die back here."

"Oh, stop being so dramatic. We'll figure this out. They're just people," I say, trying to bring some semblance of sanity back into this mix.

"Easy for you to say. I haven't even had lunch yet," he whimpers.

I twist around, pulling Renaldo up to a full stand. "What happened? How did this start?"

His face contorts as he shakes his head. "How do you think it started? The first nutter came in looking to have a word. I told them you were booked up, but I could get them on the schedule in the future. But before I could even open the appointment app, more were coming in. I practically had to beat them back to close up the shop. I even broke a nail." He holds out his hand, whimpering at a tiny chip missing from his middle fingernail.

I roll my eyes, taking a few steps away. He's as bad as I am with all of this. It's no wonder Apollo thought I needed Kyros resurrected. His ability to swiftly sort the worthy from unworthy in the crowd was one of his greatest assets. It cut down my time as the conduit for prophetic visions considerably.

As good as Renaldo is with managing the store, he's never done well when anything out of the norm presents itself. It's simply not his forte, but it's never really been needed, either.

"Shit," I repeat, realizing there's only one way out of this—and Ren's not going to like it.

Before I have the chance to open my mouth, Kyros appears on the garden bench to our left.

Renaldo squeaks out a high-pitched cry, clutching at his heart. His eyes nearly bug out of his head as he does a double-take between Kyros and me. Kyros, on the other hand, looks almost bored.

"Well, it's about time," he says, inching his way forward so he can rock himself off the bench. It's a painful endeavor to watch as each movement takes ages to get the tiniest of traction.

"Did he—" Ren begins, his eyes about to fall out of his head. "Did he just…"

Clearly, his brain has short-circuited because he can't bring himself to finish the sentence.

"What is the ridiculously groomed man on about?" Kyros asks, quirking a white bushy eyebrow.

Renaldo's mouth pops open.

I hold out my hands, stepping between the two of them like a referee. "Guys, now's not the time. We need to get this hot mess under control and I'm going to need *both* of you to make it happen."

"Oh, hell, no. You said—" Ren starts.

I turn to face him, putting on my best mom face. "I

know what I said. Look, you like dealing with the chaos out there as much as I do. Kyros loves it."

"I do," he agrees, nodding like a child.

Ren scrunches his face in disgust. "This is beyond insane. Did I trip and hit my head or something? I did, didn't I?" He raises his hands to his head, feeling around his scalp.

"The man doesn't see what's in front of him, does he?" Kyros asks, hobbling over to me.

"You should talk," Ren says, eyeing Kyros from top to bottom. "Have you seen your sad excuse for an outfit?"

Kyros puffs up his chest, but the woman on the other side of the gate rattles the door again before he blurts out a retort.

"Come on, I just need to talk. Please, Diana, you're the only one who can help—" she says, her voice reaching an octave of desperation.

"Look, we can hash this out later. First, we need to manage this mess. Are you with me or aren't you?" I say, jutting out my chin.

I might not want to take on this craziness, but if there's one thing I won't back down from, it's a challenge. Apollo obviously believes he's backing me into a corner, but I'm going to show him I can handle whatever punches he can throw.

And still get to my damn date with Blake.

Kyros sniffles, but juts out a hand. "I understand this is a sign of truce," he practically whispers.

Ren's back stiffens and his face flattens. His brown eyes dart over to me, but when I raise my eyebrows in return, he sighs in defeat. "Fine. Truce." He extends his hand, taking Kyros's offering.

"There. That wasn't so hard, was it?" I say, grinning.

"Don't push your luck, Diana," Ren snaps back, crossing his arms and jutting out a hip.

"All right, Ren, I need you to call Blake and tell him we have Kyros with us," I say, acutely aware of the fact that I'm going to need to dive straight into readings. "Kyros, you're up. Sort through the mess and send away the outliers. Only those with *legitimate concerns* are being seen today."

"Understood," Kyros says with a nod.

Ren opens his mouth, then closes it again. His thoughts are a jumbled mess of confusion and he doesn't know what to say or do first. Either way, he's fine staying out of the way.

"Oh, and Ren—you're in charge of the books. Anyone unable to be seen today will need to find a spot in the coming days. I need you to operate the booking app. Kyros won't have a clue," I say, wincing slightly.

Ren mumbles something under his breath that sounds suspiciously like, "for fuck's sake." But instead, he tips his head toward the door as he reaches for the handle. "Come on, old man. Showtime."

Kyros nods, shuffling after him.

Tipping my head to the sky, I inhale a deep, centering breath.

So help me, this better work.

I straighten my shoulders and follow behind them, entering my reading room, so I can ready the space.

Moving quickly, I light the candles and incense and take a seat at my glass reading table.

My vision strays to the clock on the wall, and I whimper.

1:14 p.m.

Please, for the love of all that's holy, let this move along quickly.

WHERE THE FUTURE LEADS

our hours later, we're nowhere near clearing the line of people weaving its way around the block. If anything, we've gained more people as the message of my return spreads around town. This is saying something because the town itself only has a handful of residents in the first place. Its size was part of the allure of Helena, but I'm now regretting the choice—even though I'm sure the location would have made no difference.

Dammit, Apollo.

"The Pythia appreciates your faith in her service, but I am afraid to be the bearer of bad news in that your request does not meet her requirements for today. As you can see, she's a very busy woman," Kyros says, trying to tactfully remove the woman currently in the front of the line.

"How can you say that? Didn't you hear me? My pookie is *missing*," she cries from the other room. "Surely that's a big deal."

"Ma'am, your *dog* is missing. As unfortunate as that

may be, Diana's been dealing with far bigger concerns," Ren fires back, coming to Kyros's aid. "So unless your dog is of national security, we've got to get real and prioritize here."

I snicker to myself. *National security*—now that would be something.

Thankfully, the requests coming at me haven't gotten that bad but helping her find a missing dog that's probably in her back yard chasing squirrels isn't high on the list.

"But—" the woman begins her rebuttal.

"Madam, I'm certain your *pookie* will turn up very soon," Kyros says, using one of his more empathetic tones. "Now, a little tip, if I may…. I've found if you lay out some swine kidneys, they'll race back to enjoy their feast. Perhaps give that a try?"

The woman gasps.

I pinch the bridge of my nose. As helpful as he is, Kyros still doesn't have a clue how about how to deal with people in the modern era.

From my seat in the other room, I sense Kyros gently ushering the woman toward the door. Ren, on the other hand, actively pushes back the imagery of swine kidneys from his mind, and takes up the next person in line.

After all the bitching about working with Kyros, ironically, Ren has spent the better part of the past few hours tag-teaming like they've been doing it their whole life. Of course, I'm sure within seconds they could be at each other again. It's like dealing with siblings.

So far, I've seen only four people who have truly had something urgent to contend with. The rest of the time, it's been lovesick women wanting to know if they're in the right relationship, old ladies looking for something missing—*pets, keys, passwords, you name it*—or guys wanting to find the best way to earn more money or advance their careers.

None of which I'm even remotely interested in dealing with today.

The objective I gave the two of them was simple—it has to be life or death in some way. The rest can all wait for another day. Or better yet, be handed off to a different psychic who needs the money.

As it is, I can only take on one more client if I'm going to have any chance of getting out of this mess in time to go on my date with Blake. And there's no way in hell I'm missing that. He's already been so patient with me today.

Taking a deep breath, I decide to take matters into my own hands. I'll choose one final person for myself, the rest will all have to go home and come back another day.

Dealing with the clientele on the front-end isn't my cup of tea, but it's pretty clear the barrage isn't going to end unless I put the kibosh on the waiting list.

I get up from my reading table and throw my shoulders back.

I'm a big girl. I can do hard things.

When I enter the front part of the store, the chatter at the front of the line ceases and both Ren and Kyros turn to face me like I grew a second head.

Without even acknowledging them, I turn to the crowd. "Thank you all for coming today. I'm sorry to tell you that I only have enough time for one more client. The rest of you will have to go home and try again another day."

"Are you kidding me?" One guy says from midway down the line. "I've been waiting here for three hours."

I turn to face him and quirk an eyebrow. "No one asked you to stick around. If you don't like the way I'm managing my time, feel free to find someone else to deal with your hormonal issue," I spit back, plucking his question out of the air without even needing to hear him voice it. "By the way, it's gonorrhea. Might want to get that looked at by an actual doctor."

His expression is horrified as he clenches his fists and stalks off.

"Now, does anyone else have a problem with how we're dealing with this line?" I ask, looking in the eye of each and every one of the people within the vicinity.

The rest of them shake their heads quickly and keep their mouths shut. Blessed relief.

"Excellent." I nod, turning to Ren. "Do we have any final contenders? Or should I pluck one from the mix?"

Ren blinks rapidly, obviously confused by my hands-on approach to dealing with the crazy. "I, uh—"

"Amar—*Diana*," Kyros says, correcting himself again. "I believe there is one that should be seen today."

I turn to him and wait.

He clears his throat and hobbles his way out the door. When he returns, a young woman no older than sixteen is in his wake. Her clothing is dingy, like it hasn't been washed for a while and her hair has lost some of its luster.

Instantly, I get the impression of a child within her

aura—a little girl growing inside her. The feminine energy is clear, but sadness and anxiety pulsate in the energy around her, and it's enough to make me take a step back.

She escaped a very abusive situation and she doesn't know who to turn to. She isn't even sure why she's here, since she doesn't have the money to pay for it.

"Thank you, Kyros," I say, reaching my hand out to her. "I think you're right."

"But she's hardly been waiting—" a woman says near the front of the line. She draws her designer purse close to her body as if it's some sort of status symbol that will protect her from any backlash.

I quirk an eyebrow, fighting the urge to tell her where to shove that purse.

Instead, I turn to the old man at my side. "Kyros, see to it that this woman finds an alternative psychic. I'm booked from now until the end of eternity."

Kyros tips his head and Ren covers up a snicker.

"Do you know who I am?" the woman says indignantly.

As a matter of fact, I do. She's the governor's sister and she's used his status to try and elevate her own. She doesn't care who she hurts to get what she wants, and believe me, she's used to getting anything and everything.

"I don't make it a habit of getting to know every gold digger in the state," I say, knowing full well where that statement will land. But I couldn't care less.

The governor and I don't see eye to eye either.

She gapes at me and I turn to the young girl. Extending my elbow, I say, "Ready?"

Her hand shakes as she places it inside my arm, but she nods.

"Ren, Kyros, please let everyone know we're done here for the day. Then lock up," I say, pushing out my energy to enforce my authority in the hopes that it will buffer the two of them. If everyone knows this is out of their control, they're less likely to flip their shit on them.

"You heard the woman, time to lock up," Ren says, clapping his hands in the air and vamoosing them with the flick of his wrists.

Those inside the storefront grumble, some making snide comments. Others take the news in relative stride, clearly planning to come back another time because they have brains left in their heads.

With the young woman in tow, we walk to the reading room. I stop beside the client's chair, depositing her in her seat. Walking around to the other side, I claim my spot and place my palms on the glass table. I close my eyes, tuning into her energy on a deeper level.

Not only is she pregnant, but homeless, hungry, and alone.

When I open my eyes, her discerning hazel gaze is locked on me.

Silence stretches between us as we observe each other for a moment. While she's not psychic, this girl—*Jessica*—has a deep level of emotional intelligence. Something that she's had to develop to maintain the peace inside her precarious home.

"Jessica," I begin, "why don't you tell me why you're here."

Her eyes are wide when I get her name right, but then

she bites the edge of her lip, afraid to use her voice. Instead, she drops her gaze as she picks at the frayed cuticles on her right hand.

"Okay, how about this. I'll start and you just let me know if I'm on the right track. Deal?" I say, softening my voice. "You're scared and alone. It's been a few weeks since you told your parents you were pregnant—"

With the word spoken out loud, her head snaps upright, and tears spring to her lids.

"Am I on the right track?" I ask, hoping she'll gather the courage to finish. Sometimes, people like her are really just here, seeking permission to speak their truth.

"Yes," she whispers, dropping her gaze again, shame flushing the features of her face.

"There is no judgment in this space," I say, extending my hand across the table.

She drops her attention to my offering and she reaches out, tentatively placing her hand over mine. When our skin touches, a vision of a little girl with dark curly hair and chocolate skin comes to my mind. The two of them are playing and laughing at the park.

"Your daughter is mixed race." It's not a question.

Again she inhales and nods. "We love each other very much."

"Then I don't see a problem," I say, knowing full well the problem isn't with her boyfriend. In fact, as her situation blossoms inside my mind, it's the exact opposite. He's been looking for her and is scared out of his mind because he doesn't know what's happened to her.

Jessica's right hand presses against her lips as she

fights back tears. "My family, they…" The pain and anguish leak from her eyes, streaking down her cheeks.

I tighten my grip on her left hand. "Hey, look. I know it must feel like the end of the world right now, but it's not. You have a very bright future together with your little girl and Jay. I see you laughing and playing together. This dark place is temporary as you shift the reality you want to live in."

She inhales sharply from her nose, blinking rapidly to see through her blurry eyes.

"I don't know what I'm doing. I don't know how to make this work—" she confesses, swiping at her face.

I nod, glancing down at her frail hand and the way she holds onto me like I'm her only lifeline. "No one does. Not really. This thing called life is a cluster of crazy. It doesn't matter if you're sixteen, twenty-something, or a hundred and twenty. Things happen that we can't control and sometimes we're even the cause of it. But what matters is that we show up and do the best we can with what we have."

The message resonates inside me, as much as I know it resonates for Jessica.

I might not want all of this shit—but what I do with it is what matters.

"Look, here's what I'm picking up. You are obviously free to choose your own path, but I hope you'll at least consider this. Deal?" I say, offering the message I receive from my abilities.

She nods, practically holding her breath.

"Sometimes those who are closest to us can't see the growth we need to go through. Loving your family doesn't mean you have to agree with everything they say or do. You can still love your family and not want to live with them. I see a path for you with Jay and his family. If you go to him, they'll keep you and the baby safe," I say, running my thumb across the outside edge of her hand.

"But I'm not his responsibility…" she whispers, tears streaming again.

"No, but the child growing inside you is. So, why not work together and see where the future leads?" I say, keeping my tone low. "Do you think you could do that?"

She thinks for a moment, her gaze locked on the glass table between us. When she looks up, she pushes a dirty blond strand of hair from her eyes as she nods.

"Good. Do you want to use my phone? Or can I drop you off somewhere?" I ask, not wanting to just turn her back out on the street without something concrete in the works.

She takes a deep breath and exhales slowly. "Maybe a phone call would be good?"

I smile at her and stand up, releasing our hands. "Come on."

After a quick phone call to Jay, Jessica's aura has lifted tremendously. An air of hope lingers, hiding in her energy and behind her eyes.

"He's coming to get me. Is it okay if I wait here?" she asks.

"Absolutely." I glance toward the clock on the wall and fight the rush of adrenaline as it spikes my blood.

It's ten after six.

Dammit, I'm already late.

GROWING NEW WINGS

*I*t takes Jay less than ten minutes to show up at the front of Inner Sanctum Books & Gifts with his parents. Witnessing the reunion between the two of them only concretizes the impressions I was receiving when I was reading her future.

Jessica's path has been altered and her destiny is now entwined with his. While it might be painful to let go of the old—it is going to mean a new life full of beauty and wonder she could never have imagined, had things not ended up the way they had.

Sometimes the hardest endings—like having to close yourself off from the people who should love you most— becomes the seed for growing new wings.

I should know.

Despite being late for my date, I can't help but feel hopeful in my own way. I mean, how could I not?

I exhale slowly as we watch their car pull away.

"Well, I can't believe you pulled it off, Diana," Ren says, planting a hand on my shoulder. "For a hot minute there, I was a hundred percent certain we were headed for an all-nighter and I'm not an all-nighter kind of guy."

"Indeed," Kyros agrees. "I must concur with Mr. Garcia. Your authority was a spectacle to behold."

Ren makes a face and jabs a finger toward Kyros. "Where did you say you found this relic?"

"Forget that. Where did he learn your last name?" I laugh.

Kyros raises an index finger, clearly ready to explain himself in detail. He opens his mouth just as another car turns up, effectively diverting his attention.

We all turn to watch Blake's black Range Rover come to a halt near the front gate of the cottage.

My heart takes a leap into my throat as he exits the vehicle wearing a sleek, gray button-down shirt with the cuffs rolled up; all tucked neatly into a pair of dark denim jeans.

When he sees me, a smile illuminates his face, showing off his dimple in a way that makes time stand still.

God, could he be any more handsome?

Renaldo whistles under his breath as Blake makes his way toward us. "If I wasn't taken, I swear Diana, you'd have a fight on your hands. But for now, I'll just take solace in the possibility that your lady bits might not petrify after all."

Despite myself, I chuckle.

Renaldo's made jokes for years about my lack of a love life, but for the first time in forever, I can't help but be as hopeful as he is.

A broad grin erupts across my face as I watch Blake swagger his way up the front walkway.

"Hey, beautiful. Sorry I'm late," Blake says as he reaches us.

I shoot him a confused look. "What are you talking about? I'm the one who's running late." Glancing down, I realize that next to him, I look like one helluva hot mess. "I haven't even had the time to change or anything."

Blake swipes a hand in the air. "Ren told me what happened over the phone. I told him to tell you not to worry about it."

I quirk an eyebrow, shifting to give Renaldo the side-eye.

He shrugs sheepishly. "Sorry. Things got hella busy."

"Anas—*Blake*, what am I to do while the two of you are frolicking?" Kyros asks, wringing his hands.

"Glad you asked, old man. My son Aiden is coming to pick you up. He's gonna keep you out of trouble for a few hours," Blake says, patting Kyros on the upper arm. "But you'll need to hang out with Renaldo here for a few."

The expression that flits across Kryos's face rivals the expression that rises on Renaldo's.

"Whoa, whoa… No one said I'd have to babysit," Ren says, pressing his fingertips to his chest. "I have a date with a bath and a bottle of wine. Maybe two. We'll see how I feel. Trust me, I can't cancel it again—"

"Oh, behave," I say, nudging Ren with my elbow.

Blake shakes his head. "Don't panic. It'll literally be a few minutes. He just had to stop and get gas."

Ren's shoulders droop with relief. "Well, you could have started with that."

Blake grins. "Where's the fun in that?"

I bark out a laugh. Blake hasn't had much time to

interact on my home turf, but I can tell he's going to fit into my world of weird just fine.

"So, you ready?" he asks, turning to me.

I glance down, debating on whether or not to just say to hell with what people think.

"If by ready, you mean ready to take her messy ass home so she can get changed, then yes… Diana is ready," Ren says, making up my mind for me.

"She looks beautiful just the way—" Blake starts.

Ren waves his hand, cutting him off. "Tall, dark, and fancy pants—I know you mean well, but listen, you're going to just have to trust me on this one. You don't take a woman like Diana friggin' Hawthorne on a date looking like that…" he jabs an index finger toward Blake, waving it up and down as he suggests his attire, then pivots and does the same to me, "and say *this* is suitable. Oh hell, no, honey. She needs to take a beat so she doesn't look like the swamp thing."

Kyros's jaw unhinges and he covers his mouth with his hands.

I rake my fingertips across my forehead and sigh.

Blake raises both hands in defeat. "All right, I can see when I'm in a losing situation. Diana, how about we swing by your place quick?"

I glance up to see his hand extended toward me. "That sounds like a lovely idea."

Taking hold of his hand, I let Blake guide me down the steps and away from the insanity on the front stoop of Inner Sanctum. For what feels like the first time in days, I take in a deep breath, flooded by a sense of relief in knowing I'm finally about to get some quality *alone* time with Blake.

No Apollo. *No Kyros.* No one else.

Even Demetri has taken a backseat in my mind, thanks to the crazy afternoon helping so many people.

When we're both buckled in, I glance back at Kyros and Renaldo. They wave at me like a set of gay parents watching their daughter go on a date for the first time. I shake my head and wave back.

"They're pretty protective of you," Blake says, a hint of a smile hiding in his tone.

"Is that what we're calling it these days?" I laugh.

"They both care a lot about you. You should have seen Kyros while you were gone. Poor old man didn't know what to do with himself," Blake says. "When Ren called, I have to admit, I was a little relieved that I didn't have to keep him from organizing your house anymore."

I turn to him, my eyes wide. "He was *what?*"

Blake chuckles, his eyebrows raised high. "Oh, yeah. Good luck finding anything. The old man's a ninja when he wants to be."

I lower my eyebrows and look at the road ahead of us. "Great."

"I'm sure he means well."

"Ugh," I groan. "Now I don't even want to go home."

"We could always skip it and tell Renaldo we did," he suggests.

"No, he's right. I really should take a quick shower and change. I mean, if we have enough time?" I say, turning to face him.

"Reservations are at seven-thirty, so if you can shower

and be ready in twenty minutes, I say, let's do it," he offers.

"Twenty minutes? It's only six-thirty," I say, eyeing the clock on his dashboard.

"Yeah, but we have a little bit of drive ahead of us," he says, a mischievous glint lighting up his face.

"Hmmm." I narrow my gaze, wanting desperately to look inside his mind to see what he has planned. Instead, I double down, trying to add an additional barrier between his mind and mine, so I can be surprised.

When we get to my house, I'm thankful for the warning about the house cleaning because Blake wasn't kidding. Kyros was busy during what little time he was here. The worst place is certainly my bedroom. Everything is *spotless*.

I groan, staring at the made bed and lack of clothing piles. His meddling would make looking for the right outfit infinity more difficult if I weren't able to cheat by using my abilities. Closing my eyes, I focus on finding the sleeveless black dress with the hint of sparkles buried in its fabric.

Within minutes, I've not only found the dress, but I'm showered, dressed, and feeling like a whole new person. I don't usually put much stock into Ren's obsession with fashion, but he was certainly right about this. I feel refreshed and centered in a way I haven't been for days.

Even borderline excited.

However, as I put the final touches on my makeup, nervous energy erupts in my center. Even though Blake and I both understand and sense our past connection, this is still our first official date as we are now.

As comfortable as our relationship has grown these past few weeks, it doesn't negate the fact that in many ways, we're still strangers to one another. More for me than him, though. I haven't changed much in the past two thousand years. At least, not physically. But he's literally a different person—different past, new memories...*new body.*

I shudder away the thought as I try to keep my head from spinning off on a tangent.

"Come on, Diana. Just be present and enjoy the evening for what it is. There's no pressure," I whisper at my reflection. I slide my feet into my heels, stand up straight, and inhale deeply through my nose. With a final glance in the mirror, I say, "Here we go."

I walk out into the living room to find Blake sitting on the couch. His right ankle rests on his left knee, as he leans back with his arm up and over the back of the couch. He seems so relaxed as he looks out the picture window.

I can't help but smile when I notice his fingertips tap the window behind him, just like the first time I met him.

Tap, tap, tap.

When he sees me, he drops his ankle from his other knee and stands up quickly. "You look—" he inhales sharply, "*gorgeous.*"

Heat rushes to my cheeks and I beam back in response. "Thanks."

I'm terrible at taking compliments, but something about the way he looks at me makes it easy to accept.

For a moment, we both stand there, lost in the

moment. It's like time itself extends out in front of us, as the past millennia fight to catch up.

I take a step closer and he exhales slowly. Uncertainty and excitement sparkle in Blake's eyes. Reaching up, I run my right hand across his jawline. His dimple appears as I slowly drag my fingertips across his lips.

Things have been so hectic since we left Greece. Hell, even before that. But right now, I could get lost in those brown eyes and beautiful lips.

"Keep doing that and I won't want to leave, you know," Blake whispers, his voice full of gravel.

"There are worse things," I purr, staring into his eyes and matching the intensity.

He clears his throat, closing the distance between us. The warmth of his hands makes me shudder as he places them on my upper arms. I could get lost in his touch, in his clean smell of aftershave and cologne.

Who needs food?

I drop my hand to the top button of his shirt and tug him in closer. Sparks fly as our lips touch, igniting the passion between us that's been simmering under the surface for far too long.

Blake groans, planting his hands against my lower back and pressing my body against his.

Desire erupts through me and all intention of leaving the house escapes my mind. Instead, all I can think about is his touch and how desperately I've missed it. And how much I want more of it.

Suddenly, my stomach growls traitorously. Not just any kind of growl, either. The kind that reminds me I've had such an intense day, I didn't even stop to eat lunch.

Blake laughs softly, breaking our kiss to rest his forehead against mine. "Onward?"

I groan. "Do we have to?"

"I think your stomach says yes," he says, holding out an elbow.

I loop my arm through his, irritated at my stomach for not being as impervious as the rest of me. "All right, let's do this, then."

Blake's smile is infectious as he leads me toward the front door.

Suddenly, an extreme feeling of dread reaches me and I stop in my tracks. "Oh, no…"

Blake's eyebrows furrow with a silent question. He doesn't have to wait long for the answer.

A loud thudding echoes through the house as Detective Radovich knocks on the door. Something has gone terribly wrong with Jonas Fletcher and Dan's here to take me with him.

DETOUR

*T*he entire mood evaporates in an instant and I don't have to be a psychic to know it's not likely to come back tonight.

"Dammit," I mutter, dropping my arm from Blake. I take a step out in front and open the front door.

Dan stands there, his hand in his blond hair, making it stick up in various directions. He's dressed in his ordinary street clothes, jeans, and a t-shirt—nothing like his daytime detective wardrobe.

"Thank god you're here. We've got a problem," Dan says, walking forward into the small entryway. He catches a glimpse of Blake, then notices my outfit. "Oh shit, were you going out?"

I swing the front door closed behind him. "Yeah, actually."

He stands there for a moment with an uncomfortable look on his face as he crams his hands into his pockets. His mind flits through thoughts so fast, I can't seem to cling onto a single one long enough to know what this is fully about.

I clear my throat and step between the two men. Introductions are in order if we're going to get anywhere. "Dan, this is Blake. Blake, Dan." I motion to each, so they can try to get over whatever socially awkward vibes are lingering predominant in the air.

Blake's the first to crack, stepping forward and extending his hand. "Hey, nice to meet you. Blake Wilson."

Dan shakes his hand and says, "Dan Radovich, Helena PD."

"Ah," Blake says, tipping his head in acknowledgment.

I shoot him a sideways glance, knowing full-well what he thinks of the cops in this town. Then, I return a pointed stare to Dan. "What do you need, Dan?"

"Okay, look," he exhales a quick breath and runs his right hand along the back of his neck. "I need your help right now. I wish I could say it would be quick, but I can't make any promises. I honestly don't know what I'm up against."

"What's going on?" Blake asks, his dark eyebrows tugging down as his interest is piqued.

Dan gives me a quick glance and his mind is just short of begging me to allow him to speak freely or excuse myself so we can talk in private.

I nod. "It's okay. Whatever you have to say, you can say in front of him."

"Okay, cool." Glancing at Blake, then back to me, Dan continues, "I went over to check on Jonas Fletcher a few minutes ago and see if we could set up a time for you to meet with his family. When I got there, everyone was in hysterics. Someone had hacked into the kid's laptop and sent a threatening message to him. I feel like we better get a handle on this situation. *Fast.*"

"What did the message say?" Blake asks before I can get the words out myself.

Blake knows nothing about this case. I haven't had the chance to fill him in about Jonas—but none of that matters. Knowing someone could be in danger is all he needs to start hunting for his own set of clues.

My lips slide into a lopsided grin.

Dan's forehead creases as he assesses Blake. "Uh…"

"It's okay, Dan. Blake is the PI I was working with last month," I say, knowing that should put Dan's mind at ease. "He might be able to help."

"Ah, that explains the comment earlier," he says, nodding to himself. After a moment of contemplation, he continues, "All right. Maybe it wouldn't hurt to have another set of ears and eyes on this one. If Diana trusts you, then so do I."

"I appreciate that," Blake says, his expression stern and expectant.

"The message said, *'We know what you've done and we expect you to comply.'*"

Blake narrows his eyes. "Sounds like kids trying to get under this Jonas's skin. How old is he?"

"He's fourteen, but I don't think that's what this is. At least, it's not the vibe I'm getting," I say, tilting my head to the side as I try to sense the intention behind the message.

Unfortunately, the moment I think I may have something, the sensation or vibration of it slips away like a dream the moment you wake up. A strange fog settles around everything the more I concentrate.

"Hmmm…" I mutter, trying harder to focus.

"Diana's right. There's more going on here than just kids playing a prank. I think Diana needs to meet Jonas now in order to do her thing. I could fill you both in more on the way there if you'd be willing to postpone going out," Dan says, scrunching up his face.

I know he wouldn't ask if he didn't feel there was no other option.

Turning to Blake I know I don't even have to ask. The moment he heard fourteen-year-old boy, he was ready to roll out. But I say the words anyway.

"What do you think?"

"Better get changed," he says with a sigh.

I reach out, grabbing hold of his hand. "I promise, I'll make this up to you."

"I'm going to hold you to that," he says, his dimple almost making an appearance.

Turning on my heel, which isn't easy in these shoes, I stalk back to my bedroom to change into something more comfortable. My standard ripped-up jeans, combat boots, and zombie unicorn t-shirt will do just fine. It has just the right balance between sardonic and ironic that might put a fourteen-year-old at ease. Or it could freak him out even more.

Could go either way.

Again, I use my gifts to locate the elements to put the outfit together. Good thing, too, because I never would have found the t-shirt. Kyros had folded it up and put it in the back of my closet. Clearly, not as amused with it as I am.

I shrug out of my sparkly dress with a sense of wistful disappointment. Both Blake and I deserve some alone time, but it doesn't seem like the universe wants to play nice.

Grabbing my leather jacket, I throw it on and walk out.

"Ready to go?" I say, scooping my hair out of the confines of the jacket collar.

Blake exits the kitchen with a couple of cheese sticks and two packages of Pop-tarts. "You have absolutely nothing in your house that's edible." He extends his hand, giving me the combo as if it will somehow appease the angry growls in my stomach.

He's not wrong.

"You take such good care of me," I say, bending forward and kissing him on the cheek.

"I think any nutritionist worth their salt would have to disagree with that statement," he mutters, shaking his head. He rips off the plastic wrapper to his cheese stick and tosses it into the garbage bin as he continues with me to the front door.

When Dan sees us, he makes for the front door, opening it so we can all exit. I lock up as the guys head down to Dan's BMW 3 series unmarked patrol car. Blake opens the front passenger door for me and I brush my hand against his face before taking a seat. Then he hops in the back, leaning in-between the front seats to get the full scoop.

The drive to the Fletcher abode only takes ten

minutes, but it's enough time to fill Blake in on the details of the case. By the time we pull up in the driveway, he knows as much as I do without being able to read the situation.

That's one part of my ability that's always annoyed me. Sometimes information comes easy and sometimes it requires a direct connection. There doesn't seem to be a rhyme or reason to it.

Maybe it's just to remind me I'm not omnipotent.

Either way, it sucks.

Once Dan parks the car, I take a deep breath allowing my gaze to soften. Staring into the illuminated areas of the garage made light by his headlights, I extend my abilities out, trying to get a feel for the home and any of the energies that have come in contact with the location or its residents.

Almost immediately, the same strange sensation from before washes over me—like a gray haze that falls in the middle of a swampy field late at night.

"Someone doesn't want me to see what they're up to," I whisper, narrowing my gaze as I concentrate harder.

"Why don't we get you inside? You might be able to get a better read on things if you actually get to meet this kid," Blake says, placing a hand on my shoulder.

"Yeah, okay." I nod, still trying to push my senses through the dense fog.

Before I know it, Blake has my car door open and is pulling me from the seat by grabbing hold of my hand. I follow after them, my head swimming in a trippy sort of soup, but I shake it away by the time we reach the front door.

Dan knocks three times, waits a beat, then knocks three more times. After a moment, the deadbolt clicks and the door opens a few inches. A woman's face appears in the shadows. Her features remind me instantly of Jonas's and without a doubt, I know this is his mother.

"Dan, I'm so glad you're back. We've managed to calm Jonas down, but we don't know what to do. Is this—" she glances in my direction, her brown eyes full of hope.

"Miriam, this is Diana Hawthorne," he says, nodding. "And this is her—" He turns to Blake.

"Blake Wilson. I'm a private investigator. Diana thought I should come along," he says, stepping forward and extending his hand to Miriam.

She narrows her eyes but shakes his hand quickly. "Well, please—*come in*. I don't want you all to be standing out here." Miriam ushers us all inside and locks three separate locks on the door. When everything is secure, she turns back to us. "Let's get you to Jonas. He's anxious to see if you can help."

Leading the way, we follow her from the narrow entry to a larger open living space off to the right. The curtains are all drawn, and the lights are dimmed low, but we can make out on the large, overstuffed couch Jonas sitting with someone I instantly know is his father.

"Jonas, sweetie. Detective Radovich is back and he's brought Ms. Hawthorne," Miriam says, lowering her voice to practically a whisper.

Jonas turns, facing toward us.

His father stands up as we make our way around the edge of the couch and he extends a large hand. "Hi, I'm

John. Jonas's father. Thanks for coming. We appreciate it."

I take his hand in mine, giving it a shake and hoping I'll be able to get a read on the situation through our contact. Unfortunately, the only thing I pick up on is his protectiveness for his son and desperation to make everything better.

"No problem," I say, trying to keep my tone light.

Dropping John's hand, I make my way to Jonas and crouch down beside him. He sits on the couch with a blanket over his lap and if I didn't know about his disability, he looks like any other teenager—blue hoodie with the hood pulled up over his head and slightly skittish energy.

"Hey there, Jonas. I hear you've had a pretty freaky night, huh?" I say, diving straight into it.

He snickers, his dark eyes surveying me with a sense of wonder and curiosity I don't typically see in a kid his age. "Could say that."

"Wanna tell me about it?" I ask.

He glances up, noticing Blake. "Who's the guy?"

"Don't worry about him. He's with me. His name is Blake," I say, trying to keep him focused on me.

"You trust him?" he asks, his face stern.

I glance over my shoulder at Blake. "With my entire life. *Yes*."

Jonas's gaze remains on Blake for a moment. Then, when he seems satisfied, he returns his attention to me.

Extending a hand out to him, I ask, "Do you mind?"

I may not have gotten much off of his father, but the energy in the room is rising. The hairs on the back of my neck are beginning to prickle and that typically means I'm about to get some enlightenment.

Biting his lower lip, he holds out his hand. When he places it in mine, the effect is immediate. Jonas may have some physical issues, but he has an ability charged with too much power for his young body.

I glance up at him in awe. "You can sense other beings with powers?"

He holds his breath for a moment, then without a word, he nods.

"Jonas—" his mother gasps, clearly surprised by his confession. She knew all along but didn't know how to tell Dan without making it sound crazy.

I glance over my shoulder at the others. Both men narrow their eyes, clearly not understanding of the significance of this. We live in a supernatural world. The people who are in the know see it everywhere. But to the people who don't, well, it's a mundane world. The only thing magical in their life is how they can surf the internet from their new voice-operated devices.

There are plenty of people who would want to keep it that way. But there are also plenty of people who would kill to know how to locate those with special abilities. Even without getting a good read on things, I am willing to bet we're up against the latter.

"That must be pretty scary at times," I say, realizing this is what it's all about.

"It wasn't. Not until recently." He shrugs. "Came in handy more than anything."

"I bet. Could you sense me? Is that how you knew I'd be able to help?" I ask, still holding onto him. I stroke my thumb against the back of his hand, trying to soothe him and continue our connection in case I get more.

"I've been able to sense you before I even knew who you were," he says.

"So you don't get a feel for who they are? Just that they have power?" I say, trying to understand the source of his gift.

He nods. "Something like that. I get a sort of reading in the back of my mind, like a weird Google map. Like, I can tell where other supes are based on the way their energy feels. Sometimes I tell what kind of powers they have based on the color I sense from them. Like, I know there's a vampire down the road and a shifter who lives in the apartment building downtown."

"Ah, that makes sense," I say.

"I don't know what he is though." Jonas tips his chin toward Blake.

"He's different," I say. It's not really my place to tell everyone that Blake's been god-touched and has the gift to be reincarnated over and over.

"You can say that again," Jonas says, eyeing him again.

"Look, Jonas, we need to figure out what's going on. Do you have any idea who's been following you or sending those messages?" Dan asks, clearly wanting to get back to the matter at hand.

Jonas opens his mouth to say something, but suddenly, my vision drops away and it's replaced with an entirely different scene. I'm no longer kneeling beside the couch, holding onto Jonas's hand. Instead, I'm in a dark hallway with flickering fluorescent lighting.

At the opposite end of the hallway is a room with an

incredible amount of computer monitors—something Aiden would likely drool over.

"We're going to need to make a move on the kid tonight. The cops have gotten involved and if they start nosing around, shit could go sideways. We can't jeopardize the plan," a man says from inside the room, his voice floating into the hallway.

"Agreed. I'll mobilize the unit," another man says, picking up a phone.

With that, I'm ripped out of the scene and back into the present.

In a quick motion, I'm back on my feet. "Dan, we need to move everyone. *Now*," I say, trying hard to hide the terror in my voice and failing miserably.

"What is it? What did you see?" he asks, his blue eyes wide.

I bite back my trepidation. "You were right, Dan. Whoever is after Jonas—they're coming for him and we don't have much time."

"What do you mean? Who's coming for him?" Miriam says, her voice suddenly an octave higher.

"I don't know. I can't get a clear read on them," I say shaking my head. The more I try to bring *the who* into focus, the more the fog closes in. "Whoever they are, they're intentionally blocking me from being able to see them. I get snippets, but that's as far as it goes. They're deep into magic we haven't seen for a long time. Magic that can shield them from people like me."

"Not good," Blake says, his dark eyes glinting with the same alarm flaring to life within me.

I nod in agreement.

Dan steps forward. "We have a safe house not far from here. We should move you all now while we have the upper hand."

"That would be wise. Whatever it is they think Jonas did—*or might do*—they aren't willing to wait any longer," I say, running scenarios in my mind. Every time I try to access Jonas's immediate future, I see it flipping through my head like an aimless Rolodex.

"Do we have time to get some things together? Or—?" Miriam begins but cuts off when she faces me.

The room starts to spin and my skull suddenly feels like it's in a vice. My hands fly to either side of my head as I drop to my knees as a high-pitched squeal pierces through every cell of my body, consuming my entire awareness.

SORCERY MASQUERADING

It takes everything I have to fight back the urge to be sick. I feel a hand on my back, probably Blake's, but I can't bring myself to open my eyes.

"Diana, what is it?" Blake asks, his voice an anchor in the storm of my mind. "What's wrong?"

I swallow hard and try to force the words to come out of my mouth as quickly as I can, but it's hard to focus. "Something…is…interfering…"

Before I can say anything else, an explosion at the front door rocks us all backward. I land hard on my backside, and my upper body slams into Blake. Screams erupt, alongside shouts and orders.

The room tilts and all the words jumble together. I can't make sense of any of it, but I know I have to find Jonas. I need to make sure he's safe. Forcing my body to do my bidding, I manage to get up on all fours. But as soon as I attempt to stand, my vision swims and my stomach lurches. I drop back down, riding the wave.

Commotion surrounds me, but I can't grab onto any

clarity. People and things blur together, but I don't know who or what is going on. Instead, it's like standing in the middle of a tornado, trying to focus on the objects flying around me. It all zips by too fast.

"Over there," I hear someone say. At least, I think that's what they said.

Blake, maybe? Or was it Dan?

"On it," is the response.

Another crash echoes to the left and I duck down, covering my head. Footsteps shuffle beside me, then a heavy thump, followed by a scuffle. Dropping my hands again, I crawl my way forward to where I think Jonas is. I need to make contact with him. There's not a whole helluva lot else I can do until this intense vertigo vanishes.

It only takes me a moment to know I'm in the right place. My right hand touches the soft fabric of his blanket that cascades from his lap and onto the floor. Following it up, I'm met by his cold hand, as he latches onto mine and squeezes tight.

"Stay down," I mutter, the words garbled and sluggish. I reach up, trying to get him to hunch as far down into the couch as possible.

I focus on the sensation of his hand, allowing him to anchor me to the here and now. I'll be able to keep the panic welling up inside me at bay as long as I can keep tabs on him. The rest will have to be up to Blake and Dan. Shifting to a seated position, I pull my legs into my body. I tighten my eyes, trying to drown out the cacophony swirling inside my brain.

Shots are fired somewhere to the right and Jonas's hand squeezes mine tighter. I hold on, feeling his fingers tremble in mine as we both sit there, completely incapable of defending ourselves.

There's a scuffle behind us, then I think I make out footsteps, but I can't be sure.

"We'll…be…okay," I say, hoping to lend some comfort to Jonas. God knows I could use some comfort right now, too.

A bright burst of energy erupts inside the room and suddenly, like a curtain has been pulled back, the intense interference blocking out my mind is lifted. The high-pitched squeal cuts off and the vertigo vanishes like it never even existed.

I exhale as the relief washes over me. Opening my eyes, the first thing I see is Blake standing over a woman's body sprawled out on the floor. Her dark black hair is splayed out across the carpet in inky waves.

The next thing I see is Kyros standing in the large archway between the living room and blown out shards of the front door. In one hand is a can of Redbull, the other a limp piece of pepperoni pizza. His blue eyes are wide with fright as he stands completely still. The cheese from his pizza slides off his slice landing in a soft splat on the hardwood floor.

"What in the—?" I say, attempting to stand. Jonas grips my hand, not wanting to let me go. I drop back down, maintaining contact.

"Glad to have you back," Blake says, exhaling a jagged breath.

"Is she—?" I point to the woman on the floor, unable to sense whether or not she's alive. The ordinary frequencies of the room might be back, but my brain still feels too fuzzy to access my gifts.

"No, just knocked her out, but I don't wanna be around when she comes to. She has a nasty side," Blake says, flipping the woman onto her front. He reaches over to one of the lamps on an end table and smashes it on the ground. Then he removes the cord and ties the woman's arms and legs behind her back.

I run my fingertips across my forehead, trying to clear away the cobwebs.

"Master Wilson was quite heroic," Kyros says, still standing like a statue with his naked pizza and can in the same position.

We never got past Kyros trying to call Blake Anastasios. I'm not ready to unpack the 'Master Wilson' thing, so, I turn from him back to Blake.

"I figured she was the cause of your problems. She was manipulating some sort of energetic ball between her hands. I hoped that if I could take her out, whatever she was doing would go out with her. Glad to see I was right," Blake says, walking over to me. He kneels, patting Jonas on the knee. "You were a trooper, kid."

"I just about shit myself," Jonas blurts out.

Blake huffs a laugh. "Yeah, that makes two of us."

I glance around, realizing for the first time Dan is missing, along with Jonas's parents. "What happened to Dan? The Fletchers?"

"Mom's over there," Jonas says, pointing to a large armchair to our right that's tipped over on its back.

Patting him on his hand, I release his grip and walk over to the chair, only to find Miriam on the floor.

Rushing over, I drop down and check for a pulse. Thankfully, it beats strong against my fingertips. Resting back on my haunches, I breathe a sigh of relief.

"She's okay," I say.

"As soon as shots were fired, she passed out," Jonas says. "She can't handle that kind of action. You should have seen her trying to watch Avengers with us."

"Oh, Master Pollard and I were just watching that motion picture," Kyros says, dropping his hands for the first time.

"Who is that guy? He feels...*off*," Jonas says, making a face.

Clearly, Aiden has been indoctrinating Kyros into the wild world of movies. This doesn't bode well for my sanity.

"He's a friend," I say, quirking an eyebrow at Kyros. "And at least your mother's reaction kept her safe, by the looks of it, Jonas."

"True dat," he says, nodding.

I turn to Blake. "What about the others? How many forced their way in?"

"There were two others. Dan and John went after them," Blake says, standing up. "It freaked them out when Kyros appeared. They weren't expecting it. Not that any of us do, really. I think we should get the hell out of here and regroup. Who knows if there will be reinforcements."

I nod. "Agreed."

Reaching down, I nudge Miriam, trying to wake her. After a few tries, her eyes flutter open and she bolts upright.

"Jonas?" she squeaks.

"Mom, I'm fine," he says, waving from the couch.

Miriam clutches at her chest, breathing deeply. Her eyes drift closed as she inhales and exhales. "Oh, thank god." Her words are so soft, I can barely hear them.

"We need to get you both out of here and get somewhere safe," I say, helping Miriam stand up.

"Where's John? Is he okay?" she asks, glancing around the room.

Blake shakes his head. "We don't know. He and Dan went after the other two."

"Oh my god," she says, groping again at her heart.

"I'm sure he's fine," I say, patting her on her shoulder. "He's with Detective Radovich."

Her eyes betray her as she nods. She wants to believe that all will be well, but being with Dan isn't enough to guarantee his safety, and she knows it.

"Come on, kid. Let's get you out of here," Blake says, reaching a hand out to Jonas. "Do you need me to carry you?"

Miriam stands up, maneuvering Jonas's wheelchair over to the couch. In a couple of quick movements, Jonas is in his seat and ready to rock and roll.

"Do you have a vehicle we can use?" Blake asks, making his way around the other side of the couch. He pulls his gun from under his shirt, sweeping the area, just in case.

I could have told him the area is clear, though. My gifts are gradually coming back online. Energy-wise, there's no sign of Dan and John, or anyone else for that matter. At least, not within the vicinity.

"It's in the garage," Miriam says, pointing to a door across from the archway.

Blake leads the way, moving past Kyros to the hallway. He holds up a hand to us as we gather in the debris. "Let me check it over quick."

He swings the door open and flips on the light. The fluorescents spring to life, showcasing a small silver Buick and a blue Chrysler Pacifica.

"Take the van," Miriam says, grabbing keys from a small table beside the door. She presses a button and the back opens. Then a ramp extends outward toward the garage door.

Without hesitation, Jonas rolls down the ramp and heads to the vehicle.

"Nice trick," Blake says, nodding his head in approval.

Kyros stands to the side, his mouth falling open. "The sheer level of sorcery masquerading as ordinary in this time is *astounding*."

Miriam shoots me a raised eyebrow but turns to follow after Jonas.

Blake, Kyros, and I follow quickly after. I hop in the front passenger seat, while Kyros and Blake take up the middle seats on either side of Jonas's wheelchair.

I push my abilities out, forcing myself to clear away any remaining debris from the attack. I wish I knew who —*or what*—that woman was, or how she blocked my powers. But for now, I'm grateful to have them back. Now, we just need to get the hell out of here.

Miriam hits the garage door button and it slowly rolls up.

"Where do you want me to go?" she asks.

"Dan said something about a safe house?" Blake offers.

I shake my head, looking over my shoulder at him. "I don't think that's wise. I get the distinct impression anything tied to the PD is being watched."

Kyros twists in his seat, eyeing Jonas. "This contraption is such a marvel."

Jonas beams. "Yeah, it's pretty cool, right?"

Kyros's forehead creases and he looks to Blake, who simply nods.

"Just go with it. It means it's good," Blake mutters, shaking his head.

I chuckle under my breath.

Miriam exits the garage and rolls us down the driveway. The second we're out in the open, all of us are on alert and watching the area for more intruders. Before we have a chance to see much, Miriam floors it, leaving her neighborhood like she's been chased by zombies.

My mind rolls back to earlier in the day and the horde of people hanging outside the Inner Sanctum. Weirdly, they're not dissimilar to zombies. They were mindlessly brought to me, thanks to Apollo. If I could have, I would have raced away in the same manner.

Suddenly, an insight into the perfect place to regroup flashes in my mind.

I sit up straighter, pointing to the next turn. "Take a left here. I know where we need to go."

AN UNLIKELY PLACE OF RESPITE

*M*iriam pulls the Pacifica into the small single-car driveway.

"Who's house is this again?" she asks.

"A friend of mine. He won't be on the radar of…*whoever's* behind this," I say, opening my door. "Wait here. I want to have a word with him first."

She nods, then twists around to look into the backseat. "You okay, Jonas?"

"Yeah," he says, "wish we could stop and get ice cream, though. I'm starving."

Kyros's eyes widen and he nods emphatically. "Oh, yes. I would quite like an ice cream as well."

I roll my eyes and step out.

"Want me to come with you?" Blake asks when I catch his eye.

I shake my head. "No, I think this will go down better if I talk to him alone first. Thank you, though."

Kyros shoots Blake a sideways glance. I ignore it and close the car door.

The last thing I need is to have either of them breathing down my neck when I ask Demetri for this favor. Hell, I'm not even sure why this came to me as the best option, but I've learned to just roll with it when I get those sorts of insights.

I walk up to Demetri's door, and get the sense that this day is coming full circle. It started off about him and it's ending right back where it began. Sort of.

I lift my hand and knock on the door. In the silence, while I wait for him to open it, I check my watch.

10:32 p.m.

"Please be awake," I mutter under my breath. "And not drunk."

After a brief moment, I hear movement on the other side of the door. Then the deadbolt slides out of place and the door creaks open.

Demetri stands in the doorway, his peppered gray hair standing on end. Thankfully, he's got on sweatpants and a wrinkled t-shirt. "What in the hell are you doing here, Diana? It's the middle of the night."

"It's ten-thirty," I say, flattening my expression. "That's hardly the middle of the night. And I'm here because I need your help. Is there any chance we could come in?"

"We?" Demetri says, running a hand through his disheveled locks as he looks around me.

I glance over my shoulder at the van in the driveway. "Yeah, there's a few of us."

"I, uh—" he says, shifting awkwardly as he tries to straighten out his shirt. "I wasn't expecting any guests."

"I wouldn't worry about it. Right now, their safety is

more important than your vanity," I say, shooting him a knowing look.

The last thing Demetri has ever cared about is vanity. If anything, he's always gone out of his way to be the opposite of vane. It's one of the many reasons I love the guy.

"They're not looking for a reading or anything—because you know I'm tapped out," he replies, panic in his eyes.

"No, I'm not trying to force a vision or anything. We needed somewhere safe and you were the first person to come to mind."

"Well, gee, since you put it that way," he mutters, rolling his eyes.

"Oh, shut up. Can we come in or not?" I ask, shifting feet. The chill of the late evening air nips at my extremities and getting inside to have a deeper discussion would be nice.

"Shit. All right. Can you just give me a second to clean up the living room?"

"They won't care—"

"Well, that's nice. I do," he fires back.

I hold my hands up. "Okay, okay. Don't get your panties in a bunch. I have a quick phone call to make, so that should buy you a few minutes. But as soon as the call's over, we're coming in."

"Fine," he grunts.

"Fine."

I turn on my heel, making my way back to the van. When I hop into my seat, everyone stares at me expectantly. "He said we can come in, but he needs a minute.

Blake, can I use your cellphone to call Dan? I want to make sure he and John are okay. Plus, I can give him details on our location."

Blake pulls his cellphone from his coat pocket and passes it over without a single word. I follow his gaze, which hasn't left Demetri's door.

Exhaling slowly, I turn back around and face the front with his phone in my hand. I tap it and bop it on the side, but nothing happens.

"Er—any chance you wanna help with this?" I ask, holding the darkened screen in his direction.

"Sorry," he mutters, taking it back and doing his magic.

I really gotta figure these newfangled phone things out. But gods, they're a pain in the ass.

"Thanks." I take the phone back, typing in Dan's number and pressing the big green phone button in the middle. At least I've learned that much.

It rings three times and each time I find myself clutching the phone a little tighter. I still can't pick up on him or John, and I'm hoping it's because I'm not fully back online yet—and not the *other thing*. On the fourth ring, he answers.

"Oh, thank goodness," I breathe out.

"Nice to hear from you, too. Where are you at?" Dan asks, his voice rough and his breathing erratic.

"We're safe," I say. "What about you? What's happened? I can't get a read on you. I think whatever they did back at the Fletcher's, it's messed with my abilities a bit."

"John and I chased the other two through the streets.

Seems like they were mostly just hired muscle, but when they caught wind of the rest of us, they bailed."

"Are you both okay?"

"Yeah, but we lost them. I don't know if they're just damn good at hiding or if they found someone with powers to help them out," Dan says, his voice leveling out a bit. "We're almost back to the house. Are you still there? Did everything go okay?"

"Yeah, we're all okay. Blake took out the woman. But we got out of there so we could relocate somewhere safe. Do you remember that friend's house where we played poker last year? Don't say his name—just in case anyone's listening," I say.

"Yeah, I remember."

"Okay, good. Meet us there when you can, but avoid going inside the Fletcher's house without backup. The one who took out my abilities is in there and I'm not a hundred percent she'll still be subdued."

"Got it. Thanks, Diana."

"Bye," I say, handing the phone back to Blake.

He takes it, hitting the large red button and dropping it back into his pocket.

"All right, let's move inside. Be careful, though. I don't want any more surprises," I say, casting my gaze out the side window.

"I do believe we all concur," Kyros adds, nodding his head. "Granted, I'm quite certain I came in at the tail end of things, but I lost a very good piece of pizza in the fray. It was a shame to be sure."

"Mmmmm, pizza," Jonas mutters.

"We can order pizza or something in a little bit, sweet-ie," Miriam says, her eyes drawn back to her son.

"Yesssss," he whispers, pulling his elbow into his side.

Kyros nods in approval.

"Okay, on that note…let's get everyone inside. Shall we?" I say, opening my door.

Jonas is surprisingly agile with his wheelchair and the back of the van. It takes him less time than Kyros to get out of the vehicle. Within a matter of minutes, we're all gathered around Demetri's front door.

I rap on the wood, hoping he's been given enough time to do whatever it was he needed to do. Probably clean up his bong collection or something.

When he opens the door, his hair is combed and he's wearing jeans and a different t-shirt. I raise an eyebrow and walk inside without a word. He stands back, opening the door wider for everyone to enter in behind me. He doesn't say a word when he sees Blake, but his expression flickers when he notices Jonas.

He always was a softie for kids.

Once we're all inside, he shoves his head out the door, looks both ways, and slams it shut.

"All right, so who here wants to tell me what the hell is going on?" Demetri says, turning around to face us.

Kyros and Jonas both jab a finger, pointing at me. Blake edges closer to my side, and places a hand on the small of my back.

"It's not like I know what the hell is really going on here, either," I say, making a face. "If anyone should be telling this story, it's Dan."

"Dan? The Detective that can't play poker to save his life?" Demetri snorts.

"Yeah, that Dan. Look, this kid has gotten himself mixed up in something and I'm not sure what to make of it," I say, stepping away from Blake's warm hand to pace the space between Demetri and me.

"So, why don't you just use your holier than thou gifts to sort it out? Aren't you the *'world's most powerful psychic'* or some shit?" he says, crossing his arms.

I blanch. "First of all, who the hell said that? Secondly, don't you think I've tried? Whoever we're dealing with has some serious power backing their play."

"I'll say, it took Diana offline completely for a bit," Blake says, concern painted in his tone.

"Explain," Demetri says, his expression darkening.

"Look, we were brought in to get a read on Jonas here," I say pointing at the kid. "He's got some interesting gifts and I think whoever this is, they're interested in him. But I can't be sure—because I can't get a read on them. Every time I try, it's like I'm hitting a full-on fog wall."

"We?" Demetri says, his gray gaze sliding to Blake.

"Yes, we. Blake and I," I say, annunciating each word slowly. He might not be psychic anymore, but he can still pick up what I'm laying down. Of that, I have no doubt.

"God, I need a drink," he says, dropping his arms and walking past us all. He continues down the hall into the kitchen.

"Do we follow him? Or—?" Kyros asks, looking from me and Blake to the kitchen, then back again.

"Go," I say, shooing them all down the hallway.

Demetri's place isn't big, but it's cozy enough.

However, each of the rooms along the hallway are dark, without a single light on, other than the kitchen. I desperately want to know what he's hiding, but I force myself to continue to the kitchen and leave him to his privacy. It's the least I can do at the present moment.

Kyros enters the kitchen first, followed by Miriam and Jonas, then Blake and myself. I catch the tail-end of Demetri's swig, as he sets down his glass of whiskey and shudders from the aftertaste.

"What is it you all want from me?" he says, not bothering to turn and face us.

"Like I said, we just need a safe place for them to stay for now," I say, glancing around the room. There are remnants of past drinking binges scattered across various surfaces, but to the untrained eye, it just looks like normal meal usage. However, I know better. There are fewer pots, pans, and plates than there should be, knowing how he likes to cook.

"Why here? You can go anywhere else. Hell, pretty sure that pretty boy detective has some safe places," he mutters, his shoulders tense and creeping up toward his ears.

"Good question," Blake mutters, clearly as amused as Demetri.

"You know, I don't know. I got the damn impression this was the place we needed to be and I've stopped questioning those nudges," I say, fighting the urge to take a drink myself.

"Well, isn't that good for you?" Demetri says, taking another jab at the fact that I have my powers when he doesn't.

"I've said I was sorry about all of this. I don't know

what else to tell you, Demetri. But we're *supposed* to be here. *You're* supposed to help us," I fire back.

"Oh, that's right. I'm only here for Diana fuckin' Hawthorne when she needs help. I forgot about that," he says, spinning around to lock eyes with me.

"Did we step in on something?" Miriam asks.

"I'd like to know the same thing," Blake mutters under his breath.

Jonas scratches at the back of his neck. "Are we not going to order pizza?"

A knock at the door makes us all jump.

"Jesus, you really are off your game, aren't you?" Demetri says, sauntering forward and pushing his way between Blake and me. He walks down the dark hallway toward the front door.

"Be careful. We don't know who—"

Before I have time to say another word, Demetri swings the door open.

15

MAYBE TOMORROW WILL BE
BETTER

*P*ushing the door open wider, Demetri steps aside, sweeping his hand out in front of him as he does so.

"We were just talking about you," he mutters, as Dan and John step inside. "Everyone's in the kitchen. Keep going straight. Can't miss it."

Detective Radovich glances down the hall, catching my expectant gaze. I tip my chin, relieved to see them both in one piece. I don't like it when my gifts go on the fritz and I can't get a clear read on things. Even if I do know how capable Dan is, it's nice to know nothing bad happened to any of them.

The three men make their way into the kitchen in relative silence. Dan shoots a confused look at Kyros, but moves over toward the right-hand side of the room, and leans against the refrigerator.

John rushes to Miriam, kissing her cheek before dropping down to eye-level with Jonas. "You okay?" he asks, his dark eyes serious as he looks over his son.

Jonas nods. "I'm fine."

John exhales, his shoulders dropping as if a weight was lifted.

"So, I guess Diana was right. They were planning to make a move on Jonas," Dan says. He clenches his jaw as his brow furrows.

"Wish we had more information to go on. Or, *hell*, more warning," Blake says, turning to face me. He reaches out, grabbing hold of my right hand, and giving it a squeeze.

My eyebrows flick upward. "You're telling me. Whoever this group is, they're smart, organized, and have a level of magic at their disposal that's keeping my abilities at bay."

"What happened to you back there?" Dan asks.

I shrug. "I'm not entirely sure. One minute I was fine, the next minute—"

"Elira can control and interfere with sound waves. That's her power," Jonas says, his voice barely a whisper.

"Elira?" I say, turning to him.

He nods. "I heard one of the others call her that before everything got super nuts."

I glance around the room. "Well, at least now we have a name."

"So, if sound waves can knock you offline, how does that work?" Dan asks, standing up straighter.

"Your guess is as good as mine," I say, eyeing Jonas again.

His dark brown eyes sparkle with knowing. "Brain waves can be disrupted with the right frequencies. She just manipulates that to her advantage. She can blanket it, or she can focus it like a laser."

Blake scoffs. "If she could have blanketed the room, why didn't she? She could have taken us all out and gotten away before we knew what hit us."

Jonas shakes his head, locking eyes with me. "She had to take out the biggest threat."

"How did she know I was a threat?" I ask.

"Anyone with a *hint* of ability can sense the power rolling off you," Jonas says, shooting me a knowing look that only a teenager can pull off. "Taking you down took everything she had, though. Her power isn't unlimited. Using it weakens her. It's why he was able to take her out." Jonas points at Blake.

"So, what do we know for certain?" Kyros asks, stepping out and raising an index finger to the sky. His gray hair is frayed and his eyes wild. "We know whoever is behind this evening's attack is supernatural in nature. They have mercenaries that can take out Amar—*Diana*. And they are organized enough to at least get past her defenses."

"We also know they're after Jonas," I add.

"Who's this guy?" Dan asks, finally letting his curiosity get the better of him.

"He's with us," I say, swishing my thumb in the air between myself and Blake.

As if that makes total sense, Dan's eyebrows skirt his hairline and he nods. He knows better than to ask too many questions where I'm concerned.

Kyros puffs up his chest. "Indeed, Amar—*Diana* is in my charge. I was resurrected to keep her in line."

The detective's eyes widen further as he glances from Kyros back to me.

I shrug.

"Glad we cleared all that shit up. But how about we get around to what the hell you're all doing in my house?" Demetri says, walking over to the fridge. He gestures to Dan to get out of the way as he opens it up and grabs himself a beer.

Kyros tsks.

"I already told you. They need somewhere safe to lay low. You are the only one I know that has enough wards set up to keep them shrouded from these people," I say, agitated that he'd have the audacity to challenge my intuition. He should know better than that.

"Yeah, well, those days are gone. Non-magical here, remember?" he says, pointing at himself with his free hand as he takes another sip of beer.

"Bullshit. You and I both know wards have nothing to do with being magical. Anyone with the right tools and words can set up wards," I spit. "Stop feeling so damn sorry for yourself. It doesn't suit you."

Dan's lips press into a thin line and he takes a step back, diverting his gaze to the floor.

"Yeah, well, it doesn't mean I need to take on house guests. What if I just wanna wallow in peace without a judgmental crew looking over my shoulder?"

"We don't mean to be any trouble—" Miriam begins.

Demetri's gaze floats over to her, then drops to Jonas. Something flickers across his face, and if you didn't know Demetri, it would have seemed like a sneer. But I know better. It was the micro-expression of a man fighting with himself.

Eh, may as well twist the knife a bit.

"Demetri, if you turn them away, how will you feel when you find out something terrible happened to this boy?" I say, dropping Blake's hand to step into the middle of the room and point at Jonas.

Demetri never married and never had kids. It's part of what drew the two of us together. And just like me, he's always had a soft spot for the vulnerable. If there was one thing he couldn't abide by, it was exactly this sort of thing.

For a moment, he stares at me with his lips pressed tight.

"Fuck." He takes a big drag off the bottle, shaking off the after-taste. "Fine. They can stay."

"Thank you, Demetri. It's only until we catch who's doing this," I say, as relief rushes over me. In the back of my mind, a surge of energy blossoms, like some sort of energetic flower.

I may not understand it fully, but I'm on the right path. *I can feel it.*

"But you're going to need to help me fortify the wards. I haven't been keeping them up since—" He glances from me to Blake. "Since shit went sideways."

Blake shoots me a confused look and I hold up a hand, shaking my head. We don't have time to go into that right now. I'll explain it all to him when the time is right.

"Fine, let's get the wards up," I say, walking out of the room and down the hallway.

"Can we order pizza now?" Jonas asks.

"Oh, yes. Pizza would, indeed, be appreciated," Kyros says.

I roll my eyes.

Demetri rushes out of the kitchen after me. He tries to get past me, but I keep moving forward without adjusting my pace. "Hold on, let me just—"

Without waiting for him, I flick on the light in the living room, revealing a mess of bottles and blankets. An attempt had been made to straighten up, however. Newspapers were slightly stacked and there was an overflowing garbage bin in the corner.

"Housekeeper quit?" I chuckle.

"Something like that," he mumbles. "Come on, let's just get this damn thing over with. I assume you want to get on with your evening."

I pull up short, twisting to look him in the eye. "What's that supposed to mean?"

He squares up to me. "Well, you're clearly here with that Blake guy. There's a lot of *we's* and *us's* being thrown around."

"First of all, I don't know how any of that matters," I say, placing a hand on my hip and channeling Ren.

He raises his hands. "Oh, far be it from me to assume that a friend should tell another friend that they're dating someone new."

"Oh, right… Like you told me about the woman who answered the phone when I called you last month?" I retort.

He flinches. "Yeah, well…she and I weren't a *thing*. Not really."

"Sure," I say, walking over to the hutch in the far right

corner where he keeps all of his magical supplies. I fling back the doors to find the whole thing in shambles. Bottles are tipped over, items are shoved in weird places and at odd angles. Some of the items are even broken or snapped in half. I turn to face him.

He shrugs in response.

"You're a two-year-old. You know that, right?" I mutter, turning back to the mess. Digging through the chaos, I pluck out the items we need to get this ball rolling. Between the two of us, there isn't much we need, but sage, sweetgrass, and salt will amplify our intentions nicely. Plus, it should give Demetri something more to focus on than his lack of psychic abilities.

"I'm gonna head out, guys," Dan says from the living room doorway. He grimaces slightly at the mess but doesn't say a word about it. "I want to get eyes on the Fletcher's house and see if that Elira chick is still there. I've called in backup, but I want to meet them."

"Be extremely careful, if she is," I warn.

"Understood," he says. Tipping his chin to both of us, he lets himself out.

Demetri drops down opposite me as I set everything down on the coffee table. He removes the bottles and wipes back the dust with the back of his sleeve. "So, are you gonna at least explain the guy?"

I sigh. "There's a lot to explain, but do you really think right now is the best time?"

Again, he shrugs. "Won't know unless you try, will we?"

I shoot him a look of annoyance. He's not going to let it go.

"Fine. His name is Blake Wilson and he's the PI from that case last month," I begin.

"Wow, you sure do move fast," he mutters, shooting me a lopsided grin.

"It wasn't like that, smart ass," I say, leaning across the table and shoving his shoulder.

He almost laughs. "What was it like then?"

I sit up on my haunches, thinking for a moment. Finally, I say, "I think it was us. You and me. I think what we did with the Violet Flame…it sent him to me."

He snickers. "Oh, now you're just grasping at straws, woman. That's ridic—"

"I remember everything," I say, holding his gaze.

He narrows his eyes. After a beat, he whispers, "What do you mean?"

"*Everything*," I say, reinforcing the word and infusing it with power.

Even he feels it because he shivers.

"But—*how?* I thought it didn't—? It backfired. My abilities—" he says, unable to form complete thoughts.

I blow out a breath, trying to center myself so I say things in a way that keeps him calm. "It took time… It was like unlocking my memory had stages as the universe sent me the way in perfectly timed steps. Blake was one of them."

As much as I want to explain about Blake being Anastasios, I get the overwhelming sense that now's not the right time.

"You're going to need to be less vague than that," he mutters, scratching his chin.

"I know—*and I will*. But right now, we need to focus

on *this*," I say, splaying my hands over the items on the table.

He nods. "All right, let's get it done."

Both of us could ward the home with our eyes closed and no items whatsoever. We've been doing it long enough. In fact, the act of warding has been something we've taught each other how to get better at.

Despite only being half a century old, he's taught me a lot I didn't already know.

We set to work, utilizing the ingredients, sacred symbols, and our voices. In a matter of fifteen or so minutes, the previous wards are fortified and I feel confident that Jonas is safe here with Demetri. While I could have brought him to my place, my concern is that whoever is after him might know who I am—and what I can do. They could come for him at my house without needing much effort to find him.

Here, on the other hand...

We finish up, just as there's a knock on the door.

I push my abilities to see if they're back online yet. Sure enough, the image of a gangly seventeen-year-old with a wrinkled company t-shirt and rusty car comes to mind.

The pizza is here.

I glance up just in time to see Kyros run awkwardly down the hall toward the front door, followed closely by Blake.

"Goddammit, old man. You don't just race to open the door," he mutters.

After a quick exchange, Kyros walks past the living room, grinning triumphantly, with pizza in hand.

"You're gonna have to explain that guy, too," Demetri says. "He's fuckin' weird."

"There are no words." I shake my head.

He barks out a laugh.

After a slice of pizza and some sleepy exchanges, Blake, Kyros, and I finally make our way back to my place. An uneasy peace settles over me when we enter my living room.

I can tell it's niggling at both of them, too, because neither one said much on the walk home.

As much as I trust my intuition, I can't help but worry about Jonas, his family...and even Demetri. I only hope that this alliance hasn't put him in more jeopardy, but only time will tell.

Kyros walks over to the couch, flopping down face-first into the cushions. He's snoring before Blake and I even get to the hallway.

"I've text Aiden and told him not to expect me home tonight. If that's..." Blake says, his eyes lingering on mine. "If that's okay with you."

"Of course, you can stay," I say, running a hand along his cheek. "But how about in the bed this time?"

His eyes light up and a smile graces his lips. "Sleeping with you before the first date..."

"Don't get too excited," I smirk. "*Just sleep.* I still expect that date."

Blake bends forward, brushing his lips against my neck. "Your wish is my command."

A shiver of excitement rolls through me, but my body is heavy and ready to give in to the exhaustion of the day. It was all go from the moment I woke and never let up.

I can only hope tomorrow will be better. Maybe we'll even get that date…

Together, we crawl under the covers, curling up next to each other. The feeling of his warm body next to mine is so comforting, so natural, I can't help but relax into him.

I swear, I no sooner descend into the darkness of sleep, nestled in Blake's arms, when my entire body vibrates into alertness, caused by a huge jolt of adrenaline.

16

HIDING FROM THE HORDE

*B*eside us on the nightstand, the phone on my nightstand blares to life. I think about kicking it across the room, but I lean over and pick it up.

"Hello?" I say, my voice thick with disorientation.

"Where in the *hell* are you?" Renaldo asks, his voice reaching the kind of pitch that makes me pull the phone away from my ear.

When I return it to my head, my annoyance levels are reaching new heights. "What are you even on about? I just went to bed."

"Well, I don't know who the hell goes to bed at noon, but woman, I am not getting paid enough to deal with these people." Ren lowers his voice and hisses, "Remember the crazies from yesterday? Well, they're back and they brought friends. If you thank the line was bad yesterday, *oh sister*…you're in for a rude awakening today. Get your scrawny ass down there."

I run my hand over my face and groan.

How can it possibly be noon already? I lean over, directing the alarm clock to face my direction.

Sure as shit, it says 12:03 p.m.

"I'll be there as soon as I can," I say setting down the receiver before Ren can spew any profanities about the vagueness of that.

"Everything okay, beautiful?" Blake asks, rolling over and placing his arms around my waist, tugging me in tighter to him.

The heat from his body radiates down my skin. Closing my eyes, I place my arm over his, trying to give myself the grace to allow at least a few moments of peace before the chaos comes crashing back in. I trace his forearm with my fingertips, drawing goosebumps across his upper arm.

Blake props himself up on his elbow, his eyebrows tugged in. "What's wrong?"

I sigh. "Evidently, it's morning."

Blake huffs out a laugh. "Yes, that tends to happen."

I shoot him a sideways glance. "I swear, I just closed my eyes and now the crazy train is back at Inner Sanctum. Ren's about to lose his shit over it."

"Ah, so that's what the call was about," he says, nodding to himself.

"It's too early." I roll over, hiding under the pillow. Blake rubs his hand across my back, sending unexpected tendrils of desire rolling through me.

Before I have the chance to do anything crazy, Blake's hand is gone. I pull the pillow off as he slides from the bed and reaches for his jeans. As he pulls them up over his hips, I let out a soft sigh.

Gods, he has a nice ass.

"I'll get the coffee going," Blake says, pulling his t-shirt on. I keep my eyes trained on him as he walks around the end of the bed. His lips slide into a smirk as he reaches my side.

I sigh, wishing we could just be normal people, having a normal start to the day. Who knows what kind of direction that might have led?

"What?" he asks, his dimple emerging from its hiding place.

"You do that so well," I blurt out.

His eyebrows tip up in the middle. "Really? You prefer me clothed? Hmmm, I have my work cut out for me, I see." Chuckling softly, he bends down, kisses me on the forehead, then saunters out.

When he's far enough away, I lean back, grabbing the pillow and releasing a tight scream into its stuffing. Blake and I were practically naked in bed and it never even occurred to me to make any moves. I was just so tired and relieved to be in his arms. Maybe Ren's right—I'm so out of practice with any of this, my lady bits are going to shrivel up.

I kick my legs out, pushing the blanket aside. Making my way to my dresser, I scrounge for an outfit. I settle on my faded, ripped up denim and the gray t-shirt with a zombie unicorn.

Yep, it's pretty much today's spirit animal.

When I walk out to the kitchen, Kyros is belly up to the breakfast bar and Blake is in the kitchen.

"Is it Groundhog Day?" I ask, unable to help myself. It's almost an exact replay of the day before.

Kyros shoots me a look of utter confusion, but thankfully, Blake gets the reference and barks out a laugh.

"Did I miss something? Should I have caught a sacrifice this morning?" Kyros asks, totally serious.

I itch my right eye, trying to stop it from twitching. "Gods, no. It was just a movie reference." Pulling out the stool beside him, I take a seat.

Kyros puffs up his chest, clearly indignant. "Well, how was I supposed to know that? I've been dead for two thousand plus years."

"You're cranky this morning. Did you wake up on the wrong side of the bed, too?" I mutter, flitting my gaze to Blake, in search of something happy.

I sigh contently as he turns around, hunting for the coffee beans.

"I dare say not. I don't even have a bed to wake up on the wrong side of," he says, giving me the side-eye as he also turns to watch Blake make coffee.

"I don't have a guest room, Kyros. The couch is as good as it gets," I say, rolling my eyes.

I never needed a guest room and kinda like it that way.

"I have a spare room he could use," Blake offers, turning around with a cup of coffee in each hand. He slides one across the counter for Kyros and hands the other to me.

"You're pretty," I say as a reflex.

Blake snickers. "You're absurd."

I nod in agreement. "Fair." With a cheesy grin, I bring the cup to my lips and take a slow, indulgent sip. I really could get used to this pampering stuff in the morning.

Kyros also takes a swig from his coffee, sputtering

when he gets a mouthful. "I shall never get used to this vile beverage."

I turn to face him. "You know you can add stuff to it, right?" Tipping my cup down so he can see it, I reveal the creamy color of mine compared to his.

His bushy eyebrows knit together as he peers from his cup to mine. "Why does mine look like latrine water?"

"Because it is?" I shrug.

Blake scoffs, shoving the sugar and cream across the counter toward Kyros. "It is not. Don't tell him that. He'll actually believe it."

I giggle, taking another sip. "I know."

Blake groans.

After a few silent sips of coffee, Kyros perks up. "Did I hear you proclaim a vacancy at your abode, Master Wilson?"

"Wow, you really need to get a modern English dictionary," I mutter into my cup.

Blake laughs. "Yes, old man. You can stay at my place. But be forewarned, Aiden likes to play games into the middle of the night and it usually comes with some strange outbursts."

Kyros's face brightens. "Oh, yes. He was showing me *Modern Warfare*. It was quite intriguing."

Blake's eyes are wide as I turn to him and mouth, *"bless you."*

"So," Blake says, turning away from Kyros, "what are you going to do about the client rush? Have you figured out what's going on there?"

"Ugh, I'm not sure, but I have a few ideas," I say. "It doesn't help that Demetri's out of the game. I'm pretty sure some of his clients are flocking my direction in his absence."

"I can imagine," he says, leaning against the breakfast bar.

Kyros stiffens up, his back going as rigid as a board, as he twists awkwardly on his seat to face my direction. When he speaks, it's Apollo's words that escape his lips.

"Pythia, heed my words, so that they may be brought to life. Your cooperation is required by the time the moon wanes, in three days' time. Should you choose to ignore your calling, the filter for those who seek your guidance will remain thin, so you cannot ignore the rising need of the world around you."

I glance back at Blake, whose expression has turned grim.

"And what about me? What about what I want?" I retort. "I have my own needs—my own calling outside whatever...*this is.*"

"Your calling as Oracle transcends human needs," Apollo says. "You have long ignored your purpose on this earth and it is time that you take your rightful place. We have much work to do."

"No, *you* have work to do. I'm just a woman who wants to be free," I sputter.

"Freedom is not without consequence, Pythia. Are you so certain your desires aren't in alignment with what it is I ask of you?"

"I am not going back to Greece. This is my home," I say before I can stop myself.

Blake's head whips to me. "Wait. *What?*"

I jab a finger toward Kyros. "Yeah, can you believe this

guy? He thinks I should pick up as the Oracle, sitting in a pile of ruins and telling the futures to men in power. Thanks, but no thanks."

"But in Greece?" Blake looks from me, to Kyros, and back again.

Apollo grunts. "Assumptions make for crumbling foundations."

My head snaps back to him. "What does that mean? I'm your oracle—*I literally speak cryptic*—and even I don't get that. You won't make me do this in Greece?"

Rather than confirming or denying, Kyros's shoulders shrug.

"Yes, because that helps so much with lessening the assumptions," I lament.

"Sometimes, the less that is known, the better. It keeps judgment from being clouded."

"Says the one who's hiding the truth," I spit back.

Blake nods in agreement. "She's right. If you want her to go along with your plans, you should know by now she needs as much info as possible. Hell, that's *literally* how she was made. She always has way more intel than anyone else thanks to her powers."

"Right?" I say, nodding. "And now you want me to go with this on blind faith that this is the right path? That accepting what you want will be what's right for me?"

"Did you or did you not agree to have your memories returned in exchange for saving this one?" Kyros's gnarly hand raises, pointing at Blake. "All of this, was granted in favor of you reprising your role, was it not?"

Blake takes a step back from the counter, his hands raised. "Hold up. Say that again?"

I turn to him, my cheeks flaming. As much as I trust him, I never wanted to make Blake feel like he's indebted to me—and I know he would with the knowledge of how I got my memories back. And why.

"I was going to tell you… I was just—"

"It's true? You already agreed to this?" he gasps.

I frown. "Eeeeh—sorta? Not really?" I exhale a jagged breath. "Maybe?"

Blake drags his hand over his face. "Diana."

I slide off my chair, walking over to him. "Look, it doesn't change anything. I needed to find you, especially after learning what you meant to me."

"Oh, so if I was just a regular Joe Schmo, you would have…what? Left me?"

"Of course, not. Don't be ridiculous."

"Good," he exhales.

"And besides, if you were a regular Joe Schmo, I would have been able to read you in the first place," I say, reaching for his arm and smirking.

He groans.

"You know what I mean. I did what I had to in order to keep you safe. We can second guess all of it, but it doesn't change what is," I say. "And look at where we are now because of that decision. I still say I made the right call."

"Yes, it was a stellar idea, Diana. You're being hunted by a mass of potentially angry people, all of whom wish to seek your council, and now the god Apollo is giving you a deadline to get your act together. Do you not see how dire of a situation this is?" Blake says, raising his right hand to the sky and thrusting it toward Kyros.

I exhale, feeling completely defeated. "So, what? You want me to just…give in?"

"Hell no. But you can't keep this sort of stuff from me. Not if we're meant to take things to the next—" Blake's eyes widen and he drops his hand to his side. "Look, this is your deal, but I think it's pretty damn obvious ignoring the situation isn't going to work."

"I know that. But what about Jonas? Whoever is after him isn't going to stop and I can't just up and leave because…" I do the same gesture he just did—raising a palm and thrusting it toward Kyros.

Apollo crosses Kyros's hands out in front of him, resting them on the counter as we hash things out.

"And what about Demetri? Inner Sanctum? Ren? *You*? I can't leave you again," I mutter, my worlds petering out. "I won't."

Suddenly, my front door flies open, and Renaldo rushes inside. In one swift movement, he slams the door shut, and locks it. Then, he spins around, leaning against it, panting like he just ran a marathon.

Leaving the kitchen, I walk into the middle of the living room with my hands planted firmly on my hips and eyebrows raised.

Not a damn thing about this day is going the way it should. Why would I expect anything different now?

Ren steps away from the door, shooting me an expression of total annoyance. "Oh, don't give me that look, Diana Hawthorne. If you're hiding from the horde, then so am I, dammit. But whatever you do, don't open that door."

17

ENLIGHTENMENT

*M*y mouth gapes open. "You let them follow you here?"

I rush to the curtains, tugging them in tight and shrouding the living room in muted darkness.

Renaldo takes a tentative step into the room, shrugging sheepishly. "I dunno if any of them saw which door I *technically* went through. About two blocks into the chase, most of them started falling behind. Who knew these Doc Martens could be so comfortable in a sprint for your life?" He kicks up one of his feet, showing off the barely worn shoe. "Plus, it helps that Brody drags me on daily runs. I hate them in the worst way, but they must have come in handy since the majority of your clients haven't visited a treadmill in—"

"Ren," I say, cutting him off.

"Sorry, I'm just happy to be out of that mess," he breathes.

Kyros enters the living room, thankfully without a

hint of Apollo left. "Mr. Garcia, what a lovely surprise to see you. Would you like a cup of latrine water?"

I hang my head. Maybe it would have been better to deal with Apollo.

Blake enters the room, sipping his coffee like it's an ordinary morning occurrence. Goddess help me, the man can take crazy with stride.

"Hey, Ren," Blake says, tipping his chin and taking another sip.

Extremely loud pounding on the front door is a clear indicator Ren didn't get away as clean as he'd hoped. The sound of voices on the other side makes my skin crawl.

I did *not* want people to know where I live.

I'm inundated with the thoughts and impressions of at least half a dozen people—maybe more.

"Shit," I sputter, rushing to the kitchen to pull those curtains tight as well.

When I return to the living room, the three men haven't moved much. Blake continues to drink his coffee, while Ren clutches at his chest. Kyros, on the other hand, looks wildly amused.

"Well, this is exciting, isn't it?" he says, grinning like a Cheshire Cat.

"No, no it's not exciting at all," I say, shooting him a WTF face. "This has to stop."

Blake takes a slow sip of his coffee, clearly not wanting to offer any advice. However, his thoughts come at me like a freight train. He's clearly not holding them back and my mental wards are giving in to his projection in a similar way Kyros does.

This is what happens when you keep your team in the dark.

My head snaps in his direction. "Excuse me?"

His brown eyes sparkle with amusement, but he doesn't say anything out loud. His message was delivered and that's all he wanted.

I sigh, pinching the bridge of my nose. "Fuck."

Sometimes I have to make the hard calls. My *team* isn't always capable of handling the whole truth and nothing but the truth. They have certain things they're good at and there's no reason to burden them with things they can't deal with.

"Did I miss something?" Ren asks, setting a hand on his hip.

"Do not feel bad, Mr. Garcia. It happens to me quite frequently. For instance, yesterday I was using the latrine—"

Blake, Ren, and I all raise our hands, calling out at the same time, "No!"

Kyros's olive-green eyes widen and his mouth drops open, flustered.

I clear my throat. "I mean, we don't need to know about your bathroom excursions. Okay?"

Another knock jolts through me and I fight the sudden urge to go back to the bedroom and hide under the covers. Another ten or so people have gathered outside the door and they all believe they have a right to a word with me. It's like they've lost their minds entirely and they're just operating based on a preprogrammed mission —*find the oracle*.

I knew I should have stayed in bed with Blake.

"What are we going to do about all that?" Blake asks, pointing toward the door.

"Well, I know what I'm gonna do," Renaldo says, throwing up a hand and waltzing past all of us as he makes his way to the kitchen.

He opens and closes cupboard doors until he finds an ages-old bottle of vodka. After blowing off a thick layer of dust, he clutches it to his chest like it's his long-lost baby. Then, refusing to set the bottle down, he hunts the remaining cupboards until he plucks a glass out and sets it on the counter.

"Please tell me you have some soda in this ancient fridge of yours," he mutters, turning to face my olive green beast in the kitchen. "Or at least orange juice."

I shake my head, knowing he'll be in for a rude awakening when he realizes there's nothing but coffee creamer and chocolate in there.

"Diana, I know you don't want to hear it, but you need to get everyone up to speed," Blake says, taking another slow sip of coffee.

We all actively ignore the litany of curses being flung from the kitchen as Ren digs through the fridge.

"You're gonna lord the whole Apollo thing over my head for a while, aren't you?" I say, narrowing my gaze.

He has every right to be mad at me.

As Anastasios, he would have been the same. He hated secrets and always insisted we were insanely open—but it's been eons since I was able to be that unguarded. Life has taught me being open means being vulnerable.

"Perhaps," he says with a hint of a smirk. At least he's taking it in stride.

"Master Wilson, I am sure Amara—*Diana*—has her reasons," he says, shooting me an exaggerated wink.

I huff a laugh, stepping forward to pat him on the shoulder. "Thanks, Kyros, but maybe Blake is right. I can't run from this forever and it's becoming a massive pain in my backside."

As if in response, the handle to my front door jiggles. These people aren't going to stop coming in droves until I embrace who I am and accept it unconditionally. And maybe not even then...

I get it, Apollo. *Gods*, I get it.

I'm his and I need to play my part.

I glance again at Blake, realizing I would do it all again in a heartbeat if it meant saving his life.

"Everyone, sit down," I say, pointing to the couch. "Ren, there's nothing in there to mix that with unless you plan on drinking it with coffee."

"Dammit," he mutters, walking back into the room. "You couldn't even have a fruity flavored vodka? I could have at least toughed that out solo."

"Ren, I'm pretty sure that alcohol is older than the advent of fruity-flavored vodka," I say, pointing at the bottle still clutched in his hands.

He shudders, setting it down gingerly on the coffee table as he takes a seat on the couch.

Kyros steps past Ren, unceremoniously plopping his butt in the middle of the couch. His leg bumps against Ren, who gingerly moves a couple of inches over. Blake shakes his head, refusing to sit next to Kyros and opting for the couch arm, instead.

I take a seat in the recliner opposite the men, placing my hands on my thighs, and drumming my fingers across them. They each eye me expectantly, but for the life of me, I have no idea how to start this conversation.

"Diana's immortal," Blake blurts out.

My jaw drops open and I gawk at him. "I can't believe you just did that."

He shrugs in response. Amusement plays at his thoughts and in his energy. He's liking this far too much.

Ren's left eyebrow arches and he glances between Blake and me, evidently under the impression Blake's full of shit.

"I am well aware," Kyros says, blinking expectantly. "I thought this was meant to be a talk on what we don't know. Was I wrong?"

"Wait, what?" Ren sputters, double-taking over his shoulder at Kyros.

"Oh, I'm sorry. Did you miss that? Amara—er, *Diana*—is immortal. As am I. Well, sort of. I passed once, but obviously, it didn't stick," Kyros says, sweeping his hands over his body. "I'm back."

Renaldo stands up, spinning around and eyeing the corners of the room suspiciously. "Am I being punked? I am, aren't I?"

"Ren, sit down," I say, swallowing hard.

With a huge inhale, he does as he's asked. However, his expression is hard and his eyes are wild.

"You must have wondered why I never age," I begin, shooting him a knowing glance.

Ren cocks his head slightly, running his fingertips across his forehead, and smoothing his dark locks so they rest to the side. "I assumed it was good genes—or maybe a magic potion or something. It's not unheard of in our line of work."

His thoughts tumble at me at warp speed as he rolls through his memories. As much as he'd like to call all of this BS, the idea niggles in the back of his mind as the truth resonates deeper than the lies he told himself.

"Fair enough," I mutter, scratching at my temple. "The truth is, Blake's right. I can't die and I don't age."

"Okay," Ren says slowly, allowing the words to process.

"It's okay, you shall get used to it," Kyros offers, patting Renaldo on the back.

Ren turns to him, his eyes suddenly wild when they turn back to me. "Hold up. Why him? Why's he in the loop when I wasn't?" He presses his fingertips to his chest as the distress flashes through every fiber of his being.

I clear my throat, knowing this next part is going to blow his mind. "Well, Kyros…"

"She's my charge," Kyros states, puffing up his chest.

Blake sighs, raising his gaze to the ceiling. "This is going well."

"What do you mean?" Ren looks from Kyros to me. "What does he mean?"

"Kyros has been in my circle since the beginning. He was sort of my first…" I lower my voice to barely above a whisper and mutter, "*assistant.*"

Ren stands again. "I knew it. I *knew* it. You're trying to replace me. This is about being late, isn't it?"

"Good god, Ren, no. This has—" I shake my head. Of course, he'll only take in what directly impacts him and twist it. "Kyros is here because I'm the fucking *Oracle of Delphi* and I'm being called back to fulfill that role."

Kyros beams, sitting up straighter.

Ren's face goes blank as he blinks far more slowly than he should. He leans over, grabbing the bottle of vodka and cracking it open. Without a word, he takes a big swig, shudders, and does it again.

"I'm s-sorry, I must be delirious because I think I just heard you say you're *the* Oracle of Delphi," Ren says, his face still convulsing from the vodka.

"Indeed." Kyros nods.

Ren turns to him, looking absolutely scandalized, and he downs more alcohol.

"I'm telling you this because Blake's right—we all need to be operating from the same playbook. Apollo expects me to resume my role and I'm not sure I have a choice here. I have until the full moon to resume my role or—"

"Or all the crazy will keep happening," Blake finishes. "Apollo is trying to send a message to Diana."

"Hang the fuck on." Ren's head lolls to the side as he jabs a finger at Blake. "And why does Mr. Tightpants know more than I do?"

"Tightpants?" Blake says, his expression full of bewilderment.

I raise a hand, shaking my head. "Ren, I didn't think you could handle all of this." I lower my eyebrows, staring at him from under their weight. "Good thing I was wrong."

Ren sighs, deflated. He might hate being the last to know, but he hates being thought of as an absolute diva even more.

"It's important we're all on the same page because I'm not sure how this is going to impact things," I say.

"What? Did you lose your goddammed mind? Um, excuse me—are you or are you not Diana Hawthorne? Why can't the *world's most powerful psychic* just look into the future to see how it plays out?" Ren says, his words starting to slur slightly.

I stare, wide-eyed at him for a moment.

For so long, my life has been such a blind spot, it never even occurred to me I could intentionally hunt through my own future. Could I see how this all plays out?

"Oh my god. You're right. Thank you, Ren," I say, standing up.

He shoots me a perplexed smile. "You're...*welcome?*"

"Atta boy, Mr. Garcia," Kyros says, slapping Ren on the back. "Way to be a team player!"

"On that note," Blake says, standing up. "I assume this means you have a plan?"

"I do, actually." I nod, suddenly more optimistic than I have been for ages. "I'm gonna go seek out the future."

INTO THE FUTURE

*F*illed with more optimism than I've had in ages, I sit back down in the recliner.

"Do you need us to do anything?" Blake asks, his expression serious.

I shake my head. "No, I just need some time to get outta my head and into the universal flow so I can channel the future."

"This should be highly entertaining," Kyros says, clapping his hands in front of his body. "It's been ages since I have been able to witness this."

Ren lolls his head from Kyros to me. "No more sugar for this one. Mkay?" His words blend together as he pats Kyros on the top of his head.

"I assure you, I haven't had a scrap of sugar today," Kyros says, raising his eyebrow as if he's mildly put out by the suggestion.

I roll my eyes. "I take it back. I do need something."

"Whatever it is, I am your man," Kyros says, standing up and dusting off his thighs.

"Like hell you are. *I'm* her assistant. If she needs something I can get it," Ren counters, standing up, then swaying slightly.

"I need *silence* so I can concentrate," I say, eyeing each of them from under my eyebrows.

Blake barks out a laugh.

Ren and Kyros exchange a pained glance and both return to their seats without saying another word.

Taking a deep breath through my nose, I cast one final glance around the room. Blake shifts on the edge of the couch, while the other two watch me with the kind of intensity that makes my skin crawl.

Groaning internally, I pull up my legs into a cross-legged position and close my eyes. At first, the only thing I feel is utterly ridiculous—especially with the three of them staring at me.

However, as I take a few slow, deep breaths, the external world around me begins to wash away. The energy of the room, where I could feel their eyes on me, vanishes and I'm submerged into an inky well of darkness.

It's not the scary kind of darkness, though. Instead, it's more like the kind of darkness that rests in the cradle of birth—it's on the verge of enlightenment. As the currents of energy swirl around me, I pull my awareness in, honing the message I'm seeking…

Apollo, if I fully accept my role as Pythia, how will my life change?

Unlike in the past when I tried to access anything to do with my future, the pressure gives way, allowing me to step outside the darkness. At first, the light is so bright, I have to shield my eyes. But as my vision adjusts, I drop my arm to my side.

I'm no longer in my house, but instead, I'm in the garden behind Inner Sanctum. Blake sits in one of the patio chairs, his hand resting on a bottle of beer in front of him on the table. He smiles at me, then pats the open seat beside him.

Walking over to him, I sit down, wondering what this has to do with my question.

"It's a beautiful afternoon, isn't it?" Blake says, smiling. Not much in his features seem different, so I'm not entirely certain when in the future this is meant to be.

I nod, inhaling deeply the combined aroma of all the flowers my landlord Sebastian has planted.

There's a light breeze and the sun is shining in thick bands through the branches of the neighbor's large oak tree. If I had to guess, it's mid-afternoon. Maybe 3 p.m.

"What are we doing here?" I ask, turning to face him.

While it might seem like I'm here with Blake, I've been at this a long time. I know all that I see in this place is really an extension of myself and this is about drawing out the information I'm seeking.

"We're enjoying the afternoon," he says, clearly not ready to give any of his secrets up just yet.

My forehead wrinkles as I contemplate the usefulness of this exercise.

"Right," I say, absently.

"Don't worry, so much. Demetri said he'll be here soon. I know you want to get started. But for now, just relax," he says, reaching a hand out and placing it on my forearm.

My skin sparks at his touch and my ears perk up at the mention of Demetri.

What does this have to do with him? And get started with what?

I lean back in my chair, trying to play the part. "You know me. Relaxing isn't usually part of my modus operandi."

Blake nods and takes a sip of his beer. "I'll drink to that."

I glance around, realizing there's a cooler a few feet back. Standing up, I walk over to it and pull out a hard seltzer. Flipping it over, I take a look at the sell-by date, trying to get a feel for how far in the future I am. The date is less than a year out.

I crack the seal and take a sip as I walk back to my seat.

"Did Demetri say anything else?" I ask, settling back into the patio chair.

"Just that he wanted to stop by the Fletcher's house to check in on Jonas."

"Is he okay?" I ask.

Blake's eyebrows tug in and he shoots me a confused look. "Well, he's better now. But you know that already."

I nod, trying to play off nonchalantly. "Of course. I just meant did something new happen?"

"Oh, no. Not as far as I'm aware." Blake says, taking another swig of his beer.

Despite being cryptic, I am happy to learn that in the future, Jonas is okay. Hopefully, it means we were able to overcome whatever is going on right now. Or stop whoever is after him.

"Can you believe how long it's been since I embraced being Apollo's oracle?" I say, goading the conversation in the direction I want it to go.

"Yeah, it's gone fast, that's for sure. I always knew I wanted to be a part of something big—*helpful*. But I had no idea what I was getting into when I met you." He chuckles. "But at least things have finally evened out. Do you remember how crazy it was before you and Demetri started working together?"

Nervous laughter erupts from my throat. "Oh, I remember like it was yesterday." I take another sip of my seltzer, feeling the cool bubbles tickle the back of my throat on the way down.

My stomach clenches. If I'm working with Demetri, I'm almost afraid to ask about Kyros and Ren. And does this mean Demetri got his powers back? If so, he must be incredibly thrilled.

Excited agitation rolls through me. I wish I could get on with the understanding, so I know the how and the why. Ordinarily, a vision trip like this would divulge its insights more quickly. For whatever reason, each piece of the puzzle is unlocking itself slowly as I go along.

Perhaps it's in response to my internal compass?

The scene shifts and no longer am I in the back garden, but instead on the side of Mt. Parnassus, sitting amongst the ruins of Apollo's Temple.

Beside me, Apollo himself sits, his hands resting between his knees. Dressed in modern-day clothing, his untucked button-down shirt and faded denim jeans make me double-take.

A lopsided grin emerges on his boyish face. His green

eyes sparkle mischievously as the wind tosses about his dark curls.

"So, we're back to this?" I say, sighing softly. "And here I thought you were allowing me to forge my own path."

Apollo watches me for a moment without saying a word. His discerning gaze assesses my every movement and it's like being scanned by some sort of futuristic machine. After a brief moment, he turns and faces out toward the landscape.

"I like it here. It's peaceful," he finally says.

I look out over the mountainside, letting my gaze rest in the direction of the setting sun. "It's pretty, yes."

"Diana, things have been strained between us and I want to rectify that. There's much work that needs to be done, but I'm beginning to understand I cannot simply rely on your compliance. Regardless of how necessary it may be," he says, continuing to gaze out over the landscape.

I chuckle. "It only took you two millennia to realize this? Typical man."

For the first time, Apollo turns to face me, the lopsided grin still evident. "Fair enough."

"Look, you should know this by now, but since I'm not sure you do, let me make it clear. Whatever it is—*ask me*. Straight up, no holds barred. Let me choose, rather than trying to strong-arm me into doing your dirty work," I say, staring him directly in his eyes.

A full grin cracks his features. "See, that's why I like you, Diana. That's why I've *always* liked you. You have guts—and heart."

I raise my eyebrows, waiting.

"All right, all right. Here's the thing… Time has moved forward, but my ultimate plans remain the same. I foresee a world in balance. A world where the simple joys in life coincide with the ebbs and flows of nature. I want to build that future and I'm willing to do what it takes. But I need your help. While I have my role, I am not fully of this world. I cannot walk in it the way you and Kyros can," he says, exhaling slowly.

I think back to my life before—my life here in the temple. It's not something I want to repeat.

"I don't want to sit atop a pedestal—to be only accessible by those with power and the ability to make change. I want to be able to pick and choose how I use my gifts," I say, standing up and pacing in front of him. "But you and I have a similar goal. I've walked this world for a long while and I've seen its dysfunction first hand. I would love nothing more than to see it come back into some semblance of balance."

"What do you propose?" Apollo asks, shockingly humble as he tilts his head slightly to the side.

"We work as a team," I offer. "Give me the information and insights you think are important—but let me choose what to do with them. Don't keep me in the dark and try to manipulate me because it won't end well. In return, I promise I will do my best to help in any way I can."

Apollo considers for a moment, his eyes going distant.

I raise an index finger. "Oh, and I get to choose where I live. I know you love this place, but like you said—you don't walk in this world the way I do. You can come and go as you please. I can't."

Again, Apollo tips his head. "Understood."

Walking over to him, I extend my hand. "Then we have an accord."

He stands up, brushing a dark curl from his eyes. Reaching out, he gives hand a good shake. "It is done."

Light consumes my awareness. Suddenly, my awareness cracks open, and I'm thrust from the vision and back into my body.

I open my eyes to find Kyros, Ren, and Blake all staring at me with expressions flitting between horror and relief. But I don't have time to worry about that now.

The knowing of the future hits me full-force and I know exactly what I need to do to help Jonas and make amends with Demetri.

19

AN AGREEMENT HAS BEEN REACHED

"*I* will never get used to witnessing that," Blake says, shaking his head. His eyes sparkle with wonder as he stands up, grinning so his dimple digs deep into his cheek.

Butterflies knock against my ribcage and I smile at him. I swear I'll never get used to seeing the admiration in his eyes. Every once in a while, the remnants of his soul shine bright in their depths, reminding me so much of Anastasios.

Ren fans himself, leaning back into the couch cushions. "Well, I don't know what in the hell all that was, but I was ready to call an exorcist. Did you know you glow? Like, full-on *glow*? What *in the actual* is that?"

"Oh, Mr. Garcia, there's no need to be so dramatic. How can you possibly call yourself her assistant and not know this is a part of who she is? That is simply Amara—*Diana's* prophetic ability seeping through," Kyros says, shaking his head. "It is a testament of her true powers."

"Yeah, well, she looked possessed. Her eyes were white and everything. I've seen horror movies that start with a character looking like that," Ren mutters, shooting a glance over his shoulder at Kyros. "And what's with the Amara—Diana stuff? Do you have a seizure every time you try to say her name? It's not that hard. Say it with me... Die-ann-ah."

"The old man gets confused and keeps forgetting her name," Blake mutters, smirking in my direction.

I shake my head. So much for keeping the team on the same page.

Kyros stares at Blake, scandalized. "I did not forget her name. Her *true* name is Amarantham and you should do well to remember that, Anastasios. While you might be reincarnated, she chooses to go by—"

Ren holds up a hand, stopping him right there. "Nope. That's enough crazy talk for one day. I've reached my max limit and can take no more."

"Yeah, well, you might want to hold that thought, Ren. I've reached an agreement with Apollo and we have work to do," I say, untangling my legs and standing up. My muscles groan in the movement, but it feels good to be back in the here and now. Plus, it's game time. There's a lot to accomplish and not much time to do it, if what I saw is true.

"What did you see?" Blake asks, suddenly by my side. His warm hand rests on my elbow, holding me steady.

I take a moment, considering what I learned. Finally, I say, "Everything is tied together—I just didn't realize it. I was too busy trying to juggle everything, so I couldn't see the forest through the trees."

I'm still amazed that I didn't see what was right in front of me. It was so close, the answers to our problems could have jumped out and bitten me on the ass.

"Do you want to elaborate for those of us who *aren't* in your head with you?" Ren asks, holding a hand in the air like he's about to Thanos snap his way out of the room if he doesn't like my answer.

Kyros turns to Renaldo. "You don't have a mental link with her, too?"

Ren stares at Kyros, his eyebrows tugged in tightly. However, he opts to leave that question unanswered as he turns back to me. The connection the two of us have is vastly different from what Kyros and I share, but it's still powerful nonetheless. Ren gets me in a way Kyros wouldn't even know how to start.

Nodding to myself, I step away from Blake, so I can pace the room for a moment. They need to know the details, but it's not easy trusting my team with *everything* —handing over vital information that has truly life or death consequences. But if there's one thing these recent insights have taught me, it's that if I can't trust them to have my back, what good am I? I'm just a rogue vigilante who can occasionally see into the future. Big deal.

"We have to help Jonas get rid of his powers," I say, turning to face them. "If he keeps them, he'll die. The group that's after him—it goes by the code name Sentinel. Right now, it's currently a small organization, but if the future holds its trajectory, it will become something far more terrible. They want to harness his abilities and Jonas is just the start of their plans. We have to head this one off or Jonas will be killed in the process."

Kyros gasps, covering his mouth with his fingertips.

"And how exactly do we do that? It's not like we have some sort of power-removing machine or something," Ren says, eyeing the vodka like he might have to take another swig. "Do we?"

I grin. "Actually, we do."

Kyros quirks a bushy white eyebrow and Ren eyes me skeptically. Blake's expression, on the other hand, looks like he caught exactly what I was putting down.

Maybe he's been around me long enough now to put the pieces together when I'm being cryptic. Or maybe his lifetime as Anastasios and his connection with me guides his train of thought. Either way, it's nice to feel understood without needing to explain myself to him.

In fact, it's kinda sexy.

I puff up my chest, inhaling a deep breath. "We have a *god* on our side, remember?"

Kyros tips his head back, staring at my ceiling. "Oh, right."

"I hate to bring you all back to the land of sanity... Okay, no I don't—but this is news to me," Ren says, jostling his head from side to side.

"Did you not take on board the information about Amarantham being Apollo's Oracle?" Kyros says.

"Diana," Ren corrects, pinching the bridge of his nose. "Psh—I mean, yes. But that doesn't mean she..." he glances from Kyros to me, then back again. When he speaks again, his voice is elevated to another octave. "She has direct access to Apollo?"

Kyros's lips press into a tight smile and he nods

quickly. "Well deduced, Mr. Garcia. I knew you'd get there in the end."

Ren leans forward, pressing his hands over his face. "I am ridiculously out of my depth here."

I walk over, placing a hand on his bowed head. "If it's any consolation, you're not the only one. Most of this is new to us, too."

Ren groans, eyeing me through his fingers. "And yet, I'm the last to join this bizarro insiders club."

"Not by much," Blake offers. "I've only been in the loop a few weeks."

"And I'm recently resurrected," Kyros says, patting Renaldo on the back. "So, while I might understand Amar —*Diana's* true origin, I'm still making sense of this new world. So much has changed in the past two thousand years. I mean, Amarantham looks the same as ever—save the horrendous clothing choices, of course. What is that?" He jabs an index finger toward me.

I glance down. "It's a zombie unicorn."

"Ah," he mutters, evidently disgusted by the look on his face.

Ren sputters. "Two...*thousand?* I know I didn't hear what I think I just heard."

"Ren, I already told you. I'm immortal," I say, shooting him a confused look.

He stands up, staring at the vodka before walking from the living room to the kitchen. "But—*two-thousand years?* Is that how old you are?" he squeaks.

I shrug. "More or less."

He gasps, fanning himself.

"What did you think I was?" I say, mildly amused by his bewilderment.

"I don't *know*," he sputters, giving me a WTF expression as he paces back and forth aimlessly. He rakes his hands through his hair, making the black strands stand on end. "But it wasn't *thousands* of years. A hundred years, maybe. No… I take that back. Not even that. Oh my god."

He walks into the kitchen, then back into the living room. He eyes the couch like he might sit down, but the energy in his body won't let him rest.

Blake's eyes track Ren's movements and he shakes his head. "What do we need to do?" he asks, bringing us back on topic.

"First, we need to get back to Demetri's. I need to assess Jonas for myself, just to be sure," I say. It's the truth, but there's more to it than that. What we need to do is going to impact more than Jonas and his family. "And I need to make sure Jonas is on board. Free will is at play here and Apollo won't move on things without direct consent."

"How in the hell are we going to get out of this house, let alone get across town? The mob will eat us alive, remember?" Ren says, pointing at the front door.

My left eyebrow raises. "Are you sure about that?"

"Of course, I'm sure," he huffs, tilting his head to the side. He pauses, obviously listening for any signs of the people outside the door. "I mean, I don't hear them now, but that could just mean they're waiting to pounce."

"Check," I say, nodding toward the door. As soon as I accepted my new role with Apollo, I felt their presence disperse, but Ren doesn't know that.

"Me?" he squeaks, his eyes nearly bugging out of his head.

"Oh, for the love," Blake says, rolling his eyes. He saunters past me, unlocking the front door and swinging it open. He steps out onto the concrete steps, vanishing from view for a moment. When he returns, he shakes his head. "There's no one there."

"You're kidding me," Ren says breathlessly, getting up to check things out for himself. He walks straight out the door and within a couple of moments comes back in, surprise painted across his features. "PI Hotpants is right. They're gone."

"I told you. Apollo and I came to an agreement. Evidently, I needed to determine which path I wanted to take with my abilities, as we go forward. Continue with the incessant questions, as I have been and as I did in the past—or be guided with a higher purpose and higher stakes. I think it's fairly obvious which one I chose," I say.

Ren's eyes widen and he says, "What about Inner Sanctum?"

I hold a hand up. "Don't worry about that. Things will work out. Trust me."

Ren places a hand on his hip. "They damn well better, Diana. The last thing I need is to be out of a job after all of this."

"Do you ever think of anyone but yourself?" Blake asks, shaking his head.

Ren turns to Blake, pressing his fingertips to his chest. "I'll have you know I was thinking about what would happen to Diana's store, as well."

Blake's eyebrows rise, tipping up in the middle. He mouths the word, "*sure*."

I shake my head, unable to handle any more bickering. Instead, I walk toward the open door, grabbing my purse on the way out. From the front steps, I call back, "Are you guys coming, or what?"

20

WHAT IF I DON'T WANNA?

"*S*o, let me get this straight…" Demetri says, his eyebrows crumpling to the point of merging entirely. "You want to strip Jonas of his powers to protect him?"

His features are hard and I can only imagine how it must feel to him after everything that happened with his own powers. But I can't worry about Demetri's feelings right now. I know what needs to be done to protect Jonas.

I nod, tapping the dining table's wooden top with my middle fingertip. "That's the gist, yes."

"Do you have any idea what this will do to him? How it will change who he is?" Demetri asks, getting straight to the point.

I lock eyes with him, knowing full well this might sting a bit. "I am well aware."

He rubs the tip of his index finger across the stubble beneath his lip, holding back whatever curses he'd like to fling my way. But I can still feel them hurtling through the mental energy between us.

"Demetri, if I had any other choice—"

He nods. "Right, right. It was *Apollo* who gave you this insight…"

Instinctively, my gaze raises to the ceiling. You'd think after all the years dealing with Ren, I'd be used to this. But when it's someone who used to believe in you implicitly, it stings a bit more.

Ironically, Renaldo's the one taking all of this information in stride. Then again, it could also be the vodka.

Could go either way.

"Yes," I sigh, letting my gaze drift to the small kitchen window. I wish there was an easier way to fix all of his, his hurt and anger. His distrust of me. "I know it might seem strange, Demetri…"

Blake places a hand on my shoulder, trying to ground me to the here and now. He likely senses my agitation. Ever since the vision with Apollo, every cell of my being is humming, ready to take on the role I need to fulfill in all of this. I never thought I'd be like this, but here we are. It's *game time* and there's a much bigger game being played beyond all of this.

It all starts here.

"No, it's not strange. Understanding all of this actually helps click a lot of stuff in place," Demetri says, his light blue eyes distant. "But I can't help but think of the times when your best intentions blew up in our faces. *Literally.*"

"This isn't like that—"

"It's *exactly* like that. You want us, *him*, to trust you. To believe you know the exact right thing to do. But sometimes, you don't. Sometimes, your gifts are shit," he spits.

"What happened with you was different. It was before I knew what I was. It was before—"

"Apollo. I heard you the first time," Demetri says, shaking his head.

"Look, you don't have to believe Apollo is involved if you don't want to. But if you're not gonna help, then get the fuck out of the way," Blake growls.

Demetri quirks an eyebrow but doesn't say anything else about the matter.

The entire Fletcher family, on the other hand, sat through my entire exposition without much of a word. I don't know whether they believe me or think I'm nuts. Probably the latter.

Either way, they haven't waltzed out the door with their kid, so I consider that a win.

Jonas didn't even flinch when I said that the only way to protect him was to take his powers away. If anything, relief was the predominant emotion in the room—from Miriam and John, especially.

"So, how do we go about this?" Miriam asks. "It won't hurt Jonas, will it?" She wraps her arm around Jonas's shoulder, tugging him as close to her as possible with the wheelchair between them.

I shake my head. "It shouldn't. From what I saw in my vision, it was pretty seamless. It hinges more on Jonas's approval. If he doesn't agree, then it won't work."

Miriam and John exchange a significant glance. Raising her free hand out to her husband, Miriam grabs hold of John's hand, then squeezes it tight. "This might be for the best. We can have a normal life."

"What if I don't want to give my powers up?" Jonas asks, breaking his silence on the matter. Despite his worries about giving up his powers, the dark circles under his eyes make his chocolate skin appear even darker—almost sickly. He's not sleeping well and who can blame him?

"Then you die," I say, not wanting to mince words. Jonas needs to know what's at stake here because the alternative isn't pretty. But I'll be damned if I let any of that happen.

Miriam shudders, covering her mouth with the hand that held onto John.

Jonas presses his lips tight, jutting his chin out, and sighing heavily. As much as he doesn't like the burden of this gift at times, Demetri is right. I get the distinct impression it's embedded deeply into his persona. His worry is what he'll be if it's gone.

In some ways, it's what made him special—especially when he feels like physically, he's a mess.

"Don't think like that," I say, catching his eye. I reach out, placing my hand on his knee.

Jonas's face screws up and he says, "I don't want to just be that disabled kid."

"Are you kidding me? With that gorgeous smile? Not a chance," Ren says, swatting his hand through the air. "Don't you dare think like that."

"Easy for you to say. You're not fourteen." Jonas says, chuckling darkly.

"Oh, honey, I was once. And if you think being gay and

fourteen is any easier, you are *sorrily* mistaken," Ren says, casting him a knowing look.

Jonas bites down on the inside of his lip but doesn't say anything.

"You know, someone I know once told me something that helped out tons. It might help you out, too," Ren says, fluttering his eyelashes.

Curiosity fills Jonas's features and he whispers, "What was that?"

"'What other people think of me is none of my damn business.' It took me nearly thirty years, but I'm finally in a place where I agree," Ren says, planting his hands on his hips.

I laugh softly under my breath. Pretty sure I'm the one who told him that.

Jonas's eyebrows arch high on his forehead.

Ren continues, "You're a beautiful soul and you'll grow into being whatever you make yourself out to be. Powers or not."

"Very well said, Mr. Garcia," Kyros says, clapping enthusiastically.

Ren beams, pretending to toss his imaginary hair over his shoulder.

"On that note," Blake says, turning back to me. "How do we make this happen? Did Apollo give you any idea?"

I nod. "Yeah, but—"

Before I have a chance to fill them in on the logistics, the windows of Demetri's small house rattle. It's like an earthquake is about to hit—only everything inside the home stays stationary.

Instantly, I'm on my feet.

"They've found us," I say, hit with the clear vision that we've run out of time.

Sentinel is here.

Demetri is up as well, eyeing the windows. "At least the wards are holding."

"For now," I mutter, walking around Jonas and glancing out the window. A strange green and white energy crackles along the edges of the home, searching for a way to break through.

As much as I wish I could say the wards will keep us safe, thanks to Apollo's insight, I've seen what the future could hold if we aren't successful with this. Even if we win this battle, Sentinel will keep coming for Jonas. They're going to keep coming regardless.

They aren't about to stop.

Kyros rushes over to the front door, peeking through the slits of decorative glass next to the door frame like he's a part of a spy movie. "There seems to be four or five out there. The woman Master Wilson took out the other night isn't with them, however."

"That's good news. Hopefully, it means Dan was able to apprehend her," I say, trying to push my abilities out to see if I can sense her. Unfortunately, I still get mostly a static haze around her.

I haven't had the time to check in with the detective, but I don't want to mess with her again if I can help it.

Kyros nods, despite having missed most of the last round.

Blake is by my side before I give much thought to what comes next. "I'll draw the attention of the goons out front.

It should buy you a little bit of time. Do what you need to do to keep Jonas safe."

"What are you going to do?" I ask, opting to let him tell me versus push my way into his plans.

Blake shoots me a mischievous grin, his dimple shining beside his goatee. "You worry about what you have to do. I'll handle my end."

He steps forward, grabbing hold of my waist, pulling me close. His lips crush down on mine, dizzying my head. He releases me before I have a chance to get my bearings.

"Hold that thought," he whispers next to my ear.

"Anything you say," I whisper, shaking my head. Let's just hope this isn't the beginnings of a plan going completely sideways.

"I'll go with you," John says, dropping Miriam's hand to step up beside Blake.

Miriam gasps. "John."

"Miriam, if I can help keep Jonas safe, I'm gonna do it," he says, determination hardening his jaw.

Her lips clamp shut and she clutches Jonas closer.

Renaldo sighs, panic pulsing through his aura loud and clear. He turns to me. "I am not cut out for hand-to-hand combat. I'm too pretty. I don't suppose you have any need for an assistant with all of the mojo you're about to do? Because I'm a hundred and ten percent certain I'd be useless outside."

"Actually, Ren, Kyros… I do have a use for you. I promise it will be painless," Blake says, waving them both to follow.

Ren curses under his breath, but Kyros tugs on the bottom of his shirt and squares his shoulders. He's gearing himself up for a fight, regardless of how ridiculous he might be in the middle of it.

I watch them leave out the back door, not removing my gaze from Blake's backside until he's no longer in view.

With a huge sigh, I turn back to Jonas. For a moment, we lock eyes. His fear is palpable, as he clutches onto his mom's hand like a lifeline. I wish like hell that I could fix this for him without all this chaos. That he didn't have to be put in this position or even deal with any of it.

But that's not how life works.

I drop down in front of him, letting my hand rest again on his knee. "Are you ready for this?"

Jonas swallows hard. He might have mixed feelings about the ritual, but his survival instinct is clear in the panic welling up in his eyes.

"I don't think I have much of a choice here," he says, his voice slightly shaky.

Witnessing him deal with this situation makes my heart ache. I can't even imagine what this must be like for him. This sort of thing is enough to make a grown man question himself, let alone a kid.

"I'm sorry, Jonas. If I saw any other way—" I begin.

He extends a hand, cutting me off. "I know. It's okay."

"Diana, we need to do this now," Demetri warns, tipping his head toward the hallway.

I glance up and nod. "Okay, let's do this."

GAME TIME

*M*iriam wheels Jonas over to the edge of the living room. It's been tidied up a bit more since the last time I was in here, but the plush recliner and coffee table will be in the way if we want Jonas to take up residence in the middle of the room.

Outside, shouts erupt, and the rumbling around the windows persists. Whatever Sentinel is doing, they intend to tear down the wards as quickly as possible. I can only hope that whatever Blake has planned will be enough to distract them while our focus is spent on stripping Jonas of his power.

Demetri pushes the hefty chair out of the way and I rush forward, scooting the coffee table so it butts against the hearth of the small gas fireplace to the left. By the time I turn around, Demetri is already hunched over, writing on the floor with his special chalk used for rituals. With the precision of someone who's done this a thousand times, he draws a huge pentacle in the middle of the floor, then hands the chalk to me.

"I assume there are specific symbols you need to use," he says, standing back up. He walks over to his cabinet, filling his arms with more supplies.

He's not wrong. In order to make this work, I'll need to invoke Apollo and bring him to us. There are rules as to how gods can enter this realm or appear in this reality. Without their proper invocation, they're locked out from doing much beyond parlor tricks, like speaking through Kyros. In part, it's why the old gods have died out of the collective consciousness—and one of the reasons Apollo is set to change things. Hardly anyone remembers the rules anymore and they wonder why the world is descending into madness.

I drop down to my knees, drawing out the ancient symbols, invoking Apollo and his god-essence. One thing's for certain, there's no way I can do what needs to be done here, I don't have that kind of power. But he certainly does. I move on to scrawling out protection symbols, in the hopes they will keep everyone here as safe as possible. Especially Jonas.

Next, I draw one final symbol—the one I now realize is essential to all of this working as it should.

The symbol invoking the Violet Flame.

Once I'm sure I have everything in order, I glance up and wave Jonas to the middle of the room. Miriam inhales sharply, wheeling her son so his wheelchair rests in the center of the pentacle.

"Are you sure this going to work?" she asks.

I rest a hand on her forearm, nodding. "I'm positive." I take a step back, making sure I'm outside of the circle.

Pressing her lips tight, she bends down, kissing Jonas on the side of his temple. "Love you, baby."

"Mom," he groans, rubbing at his forehead.

She ruffles his hair, then straightens it back out before stepping from the circle.

I shoot a lopsided grin toward Demetri, who simply raises his eyebrows in response. He's never been good with any kind of emotion, let alone something like this. It's something we both share.

Moving on, he places candles at the five points of the star, lighting each one and whispering the elemental blessing. Then, as a final safeguard, Demetri walks clockwise around the pentacle, sealing the circle of protection with a layer of blessed Himalayan sea salt. When it's complete, a plume of white light rises from the floor, encompassing Jonas in its magic. After a moment, the light subsides until it's nothing more than a swaying cord of banded light hovering a few inches off the floor.

Jonas watches the whole thing, his eyes wide and fingertips clutching at his armrests.

I take a step closer to the circle. "Are you ready for this, Jonas?"

Shouts again erupt outside the front of the house, then a high-pitched squeal that I can only associate with Ren cuts through the noise. For a moment, the rattling ceases and we descend into a chilling silence. Closing my eyes, I push my abilities out into the yard, only to find the squeal is a diversion of some kind.

Blake's right. He's capable and can handle whatever's outside. I have to trust in that so I can take care of things in here. It's the way it's always been—even as Amarantham and Anastasios.

Shaking the realization away, I return my focus to Jonas with more determination to get this underway.

"It's okay, Jonas. It's a diversion," I say, meeting his questioning gaze. "We got this."

Another scream cuts through the silence, likely Kyros, and Jonas's expression hardens.

He nods his head, swallowing hard. "I'm ready."

It's written in his face that he doesn't want anyone to get hurt and that's weighing heavy on his decision to push forward.

Miriam clasps her hands, resting her steepled fingers against her lips as tears brim in her eyes. "I love you, sweetie. *No matter what.*"

Jonas looks over his shoulder, his eyes just as glassy as hers. His chin quivers, but he doesn't say anything. He doesn't need to. The love they share passes between them effortlessly.

"The stage is all yours, Diana," Demetri says, tipping his chin toward Jonas. His lips press tightly together and his jaw tightens, but luckily, the disdain over Jonas giving up his powers has waned. Maybe he can see—however mundanely—how necessary this is. He might not understand the *why*, but at least he accepts it more than losing his own powers.

I glance down, pointing to the space beside me. "I'll need you here, Demetri."

Demetri's eyebrows scrunch together. "I don't have any kind of power that will help you, Diana."

I shake my head. "Doesn't matter. I need you here."

Again, I point beside me.

He crosses his arms like a defiant child, but he still does as he's asked.

I nod to myself. *It's game time.*

Even before we begin, Apollo's presence is with us. The room vibrates with static energy, making the small hairs on the back of my arms and neck rise. He's been watching and waiting for his time and he's ready to make an appearance.

The room is suddenly filled with the potent fragrance of frankincense and I breathe in the familiar scent. It eases me into the power and role I'm meant to play. I may not have wanted this at first, but now it *feels* right. It's effortless—*easy*. Like it was always meant to be.

And maybe it was.

Without waiting any longer, I raise my hands, extending my arms out wide and facing my palms to the ceiling. The energy hums, waiting for my words to unleash themselves.

"Apollo, god of prophecy and foresight, divine healer and deity of truth and light, I implore your presence. I call you here this day to witness this rite and share upon us your blessing," I say, my voice echoing into the room like it's magnified by some sort of magical speaker.

Apollo doesn't waste time with his arrival. Like a storm ready to ravage a forest, the room darkens, despite it still being the middle of the afternoon. Along the outskirts of the small living space, objects rise on their own—a product of the buildup of kinetic energy. A vortex of light and dark oscillate around us, spiraling the room at a dizzying speed.

As quickly as the vortex rose, it tightens to the center of the circle, then disperses. Left behind is a man with olive skin and dark curly hair.

Apollo stands beside Jonas, glancing around the room like he's been here all along. His green eyes sparkle with wisdom and a hint of amusement. Just like before, Apollo's dressed in modern attire, with a cream-colored button-down shirt that's been folded up at the elbows and faded denim jeans. His shirt is unbuttoned to his clavicle, exposing his middle-Eastern complexion and and a tuft of dark chest hair.

Demetri stumbles back, his eyes wild and mouth open.

"It's okay, Demetri," I say.

As many times as we've worked spells and rituals, he's never witnessed a god's entrance. Quite honestly, I've only witnessed it like this a handful of times, myself. Extending my arm, I reach my hand out to Demetri, wanting to pull him back into the mix.

Miriam, on the other hand, audibly gasps, then drops to the floor. She does it gracefully, though, dropping first to her knees, then slumping over and onto her back.

Some people fight, some flee. She obviously faints when things get overwhelming.

Not at all bothered, Apollo grabs hold of Jonas's wheelchair, dropping down beside him until he rests on one knee beside the boy. Throughout the entire motion, however, his gaze never leaves mine.

I nod in acknowledgment, understanding now that everything playing out here was in some way pre-destined.

As psychic as I am, even now, I still have plenty of blind spots. However, I'm also understanding it's all part of the grand plan to keep things from inundating me. I'm only given as much as I can handle at one time.

After dealing with the horde of seekers, I'm okay with it. I've gotten a taste of what life would be like without filters.

"Diana," Apollo says, smiling softly at me as his gaze extends to Demetri. For a beat, they wordlessly assessing the other. Then Apollo turns to Jonas, resting his hand over the top of the young boy's. "Jonas, you are one of the brave ones. It's a pleasure to finally be in your presence."

Jonas sits up straighter, shooting Apollo a bright smile.

"Your gift was meant to help the world, but in the wrong hands, it could also be devastating," Apollo continues. "Your time with this burden has come to an end in order to divert the risk. But fear not, I never take without giving in return." He winks at Jonas as he stands back up and pats his hand.

Leaving Jonas's side, Apollo walks the circumference of the large circle, with his hands in prayer position under his chin.

Demetri moves a step closer to me, never removing his eyes from Apollo's movements.

"What do I need to do?" Jonas asks, watching Apollo walk behind him from over his shoulder.

Apollo stops moving when he stands right in front of Jonas. With his back to me and Demetri, he again drops down to a crouch. "You just need to give me your hand

and your promise that this is what you want. Pretty simple. But you have to mean it."

Jonas's lips screw up to one side, but he nods tersely. "Okay. I'm ready."

Apollo drops from his crouch, resting on both knees, and raising his palms to the ceiling. "Then it shall be done."

Once again, the house begins to rattle, the windows and walls sounding like they're about to come apart at the seams. Whatever the others were doing outside, it wasn't enough to keep Sentinel from attacking the wards.

Jonas quickly extends his hands out to Apollo, who accepts his offering.

With an intense flash of light, like a lightning bolt sent from Zeus himself, Jonas glows a bright, sky blue. Then, as if the light is siphoned from him, it pools in his torso, and slides down his arms and into his hands.

Jonas's eyes widen at the sight of his powers leaving his body through his hands. For a moment, it lingers there, stopping its descent in the middle of his palms.

"Jonas, you have to let go—" I sputter, taking a step forward. He glances up at me just long enough for me to repeat myself.

As if brought back to himself and the realization of what will happen if he doesn't follow through, Jonas closes his eyes and exhales slowly. His shoulders relax as he grips Apollo's hands a little tighter. Then, as if the floodgates finally open, the remaining light passes from Jonas into Apollo's hands.

Jonas's body slumps forward a bit, but he sighs.

The worst is over.

Apollo bows his head. "Thank you, Jonas. Now, for my end of the bargain…" He raises his right hand, pressing it to the middle of Jonas's chest.

Once again, Jonas ignites—his entire body glowing with a bright white light. The light consumes the entire room and I bend my arm, shielding my eyes from its intensity.

When the light pulls back, the color in Jonas's cheeks looks a little bit brighter—his body a little bit stronger.

Jonas gasps, wiggling his feet.

"It's the least I can do," Apollo whispers, placing a hand alongside Jonas's cheek. "Thank you for keeping this power safe until it was ready to be passed on."

Jonas smiles, shifting forward slightly in his wheelchair. Apollo rises, backing up to give him some room. With a push, Jonas stands, taking a couple of small, uneasy steps forward.

Without a word, he wraps his arms around Apollo's neck, tugging him in close.

Apollo chuckles, returning the embrace.

Tears race down Jonas's cheeks and he turns around. "My mom is gonna freak."

"Go to her," Apollo says. "Your part in this is done."

Jonas nods, stepping away from Apollo with tentative steps. However, each step he takes grows with power and certainty. As he reaches the edge, the light of banded energy lifts up, creating an opening for him to exit without disturbing the protection of the circle.

With his hands still glowing, Apollo turns around, extending them to Demetri. "Are you ready for your new gift?"

TRAINING WHEELS OFF

*D*emetri's gaze drifts downward, landing on the soft glow of Apollo's hands and his gray eyes are lit in their light. Confusion flits through his face, replaced then, by understanding.

"You want me to take Jonas's gift?" he asks, glancing up to Apollo's face.

"This gift isn't Jonas's. It was meant for you both," Apollo says, taking another step forward, hands still extended.

Demetri shakes his head. "But—I had a gift. It was taken…"

"Training wheels," Apollo says, shrugging. "You were meant for more."

"But this doesn't make any—" Demetri's words drift off as he rakes his fingertips across his forehead. He looks past Apollo, to the embrace Jonas and his mother share, and a hint of hope blossoms in his aura.

Stepping closer, I place a hand on Demetri's back. "It makes *perfect* sense. Think about it."

Still filled with conflict, he glances from me to Apollo, and again to Jonas. "I don't see how—"

"We invoked the Violet Flame of Transmutation *together*. I got what I was looking for, and apparently...*so did you*," I say, raising my eyebrows. He might be resistant at first, but I know he'll come around. I've already seen it.

He shakes his head, blinking wildly. "But I didn't... I liked my gift."

"This was always meant for you, Demetri. You had to be ready," Apollo says, taking another confident step forward and reaching his hands out further. "Your vessel had to be cleansed and the timing had to be right."

"Accept your gift," I say, tipping my head toward Apollo. I smile at Demetri, trying to exude the confidence I feel with this. There's so much more we'll be able to do together. He'll be integral to the team we're growing and I know that's something he desperately wishes for.

He *needs* to be needed, but he's too bullheaded to admit that.

Demetri's eyebrows tug downward as he processes.

"Oh, get on with it, Demetri," I say, invoking the spirit of what he'd say to me if roles were reversed. "You don't make a god wait, for crying out loud."

My message hits its mark and Demetri's lip twitches into a lopsided smile. Nodding to himself, he takes a step forward.

Just like with Jonas, the circle of light raises, granting Demetri access into the sacred space.

Swallowing hard, Demetri extends his arms. As their palms touch, bright purple and white light erupts in inky tendrils from between their hands. Like an octopus moving from one hiding space to another, the tendrils crawl from Apollo, latching onto Demetri's wrist. Once it's left Apollo entirely, it soaks into Demetri's skin, disappearing inside of him, lighting up his veins as it explores its new home.

Demetri gasps, his eyes lighting with a light bluish glow before they settle back to their normal light gray.

He blinks rapidly, settling into the magic he was just given. "This is...*intense*," he whispers.

Suddenly, the entire house rumbles. The glass from the living room picture window shatters inward, leaving its shards scattered across the carpet just feet away.

"Dammit, the wards," I mutter, stepping away from Demetri and the circle.

I don't get very far. The front door bursts open and a burly man with broad shoulders and no hair practically *Kool-aid Man's* his way into the main hallway. In his momentum, he overshoots the living room, rushing past the archway. On his heels is Blake, followed by Ren and Kyros who stumble their way over the shards of wood and drywall.

Miriam bolts upright in the commotion. When her eyes take in the mess beside her, she screams, scrambling away from the entry. She clutches at Jonas's shirt and pulling him back with as well, evidently not even realizing he's out of his wheelchair. Her eyes are wild and she looks like she's on the verge of passing out again.

Blake manages to get out in front of the man just as he doubles back toward the living room. Ren squeals, grabbing the nearest tangible item—a copy of Sports Illustrated—as a weapon. When the guy gets close, Ren flails his arm out wildly, getting a couple of good shots in the face with the magazine as he barrels past.

Kyros uses the confusion to stick out a foot—never the kind of man to fight fair.

As expected, the man stumbles, his arms flapping wildly, like he was walking a tight rope and he was about to fall to his death. He loses his balance entirely, landing hard on the floor.

Blake is on him the second he's down, his right arm snaking around the man's neck as he kicks himself backward, flipping them both over. The second Blake's back hits the ground, he tightens his grip and lifts his hips off the ground so the mountain of a man can't get any leverage. Instead, he dangles there, trying to gain purchase and clawing at Blake's arm.

Again Ren's high-pitched scream erupts as he races into the living room and away from the fray. He looks like a caricature of himself as he runs with his arms raised like he's trying to keep the sky from falling.

Kyros follows his lead, stepping around the two men's legs at a wide berth, before breaking into a run from the hallway and into the living room.

"Oh, my god, that man of yours is like the friggin' Terminator," Ren says, fanning himself with his right hand. "Please tell me Tightpants's quads will hold out because I'm about to give my resignation." Glancing from me, he double-takes at Apollo, still standing in the middle of the circle.

Blake shows no sigh of exhaustion as the man on top of him starts to turn an odd shade of blue.

"Where's John?" Miriam cries, clutching at the front of her shirt.

Ren crosses an arm over his body, resting the elbow of the other on top of it. With the flick of his wrist, he waves her fears away. "Oh, don't worry. John's taking down the other goon outside. That man is like a caged lion—full of manly power."

The guy on the floor musters up some of his remaining power, as he tries to flip the two of them over. Blake quickly maneuvers, snaking his legs around the guy's thighs like he's a human backpack. They roll around the floor, with Blake firmly attached to the guy's back.

"Do something," I cry out, turning to Apollo.

He shakes his head. "My hands are tied here. There are rules about this type of interference."

"Fuck the rules," I spit back, racing over to Blake's side.

Without thinking, I race over to the two of them, trying to find a way to keep them from spinning. The guy's arms flail around and his right foot arcs around, landing hard in the middle of my stomach.

I stumble back, groping at my midsection, trying to get air.

Suddenly, Kyros is in the mix, grabbing hold of the man's ear and twisting. The man bellows, contorting to get away from Kyros's firm grip on his ear. Ren also rushes forward, grabbing hold of Demetri's large mortar and pestle. In a swift movement, he brings the solid marble bowl up and back down again squarely in the center of the man's forehead.

The man ceases up, then goes limp. Blake releases his

left leg, thrusting his hip and dumping the man's body off him. He takes a deep break, before rolling up onto his knees.

"Well done, Mr. Garcia," Kyros says, extending a hand.

Ren looks down at the extended hand and rather than shaking it, he grabs hold of Kyros's forearm and tugs him forward. He wraps his arms around Kyros's waist, giving him a huge bear hug.

"That Vulcan ear pinch was epic," Ren says, stepping back and patting Kyros on the shoulder.

Kyros stands up straighter, beaming. "Well, it wasn't Vulcan, but—"

The guy groans on the floor. Ren squeals, kicking his foot upside the man's head.

Again, lights out.

I push myself to a seated position, still clutching at my midsection. If I never have to do this sort of thing ever again, I'd be totally fine with it.

Blake gets up, making his way over to me, his dark eyes assessing everything. "Are you okay?"

I reach up, wiping at some blood dripping from his cheekbone. "I should be asking you that."

He winces but shakes his head. "Eh, it's just a scratch."

I lower my eyebrows.

John walks in, blood tricking down his forehead and shirt ripped up. The moment Jonas and Miriam see him, Jonas stands up, rushing toward him.

Confusion and elation mix in John's face as he wraps his arms around his son.

"What the—? How?" he asks, gripping Jonas tightly to his chest.

"It was him," Jonas says, pointing his finger toward Apollo.

Apollo clasps his hands in front of his body, watching the scene unfold. I can feel his desire to move on from here—knowing his part in this has come to an end, but I haven't yet released him from the circle.

"My powers are gone, but I got this in return," he whispers, lifting his legs one at a time.

"That's incredible," John says, tears springing to his eyes. "I never thought—"

Miriam gets up, walking over to the two of them. She wraps her arms around them both, tears of joy streaming down her face. "I'm glad you're both safe. I was so worried."

"It was dicey there for a hot minute," Ren says, pressing his fingertips to his chest. "Blake Wilson, don't you dare put me in that sort of position again. *Ever.*"

Blake snickers, shaking his head. "And yet, you performed like a true professional."

Ren's eyebrows drop and he shoots him a look of annoyance. "Don't try to kiss ass now, Buttercup. I about tossed my cookies several times and trust me, that would not be a good look for me."

Kyros quirks a bushy white eyebrow. "Toss your cookies? I didn't see you baking?"

Renaldo rolls his eyes.

Demetri chuckles under his breath, but stays beside Apollo, likely drawn to the god-energy still permeating the space.

Apollo continues to watch the scene, his hands folded patiently in front of his body.

Clearing my throat, I stand up and brush off my pants. "We should finish this. Apollo's work here is done."

Blake nods. "We need to get these assholes bound up. Ren, can you contact Detective Radish and get him over here?"

"Radovich," Ren corrects.

A smirk graces Blake's lips and he shoots me a glance. "Oh, right. What you said."

I shake my head, walking over to where Demetri and Apollo stand. Part of me is almost sad to let Apollo go. Despite everything from before, there's a place that's opened in my chest, making room for the direct connection he and I once shared.

It's almost like Kyros—I can sense what he wants, or feels. I probably can hear his thoughts in my head, too, if he chooses to use the connection in that way.

"Apollo," I say as I reach them.

"Diana." His green eyes sparkle with the same mischievous insight and wisdom as always.

"Wait—before he goes," Demetri says, holding up a hand. "I need to know... how will I understand this gift? It seems like everything is so loud right now."

"The patterns will begin to emerge. You'll get a better idea of how it works over time," Apollo offers with a nod.

"Plus, you have an expert you can turn to," I say, shifting my gaze to Jonas.

That seems to appease Demetri, as a grin breaks across his face. "Good point."

"Well, I think our work here is done. It's time to release Apollo," I say, taking a step forward to break the circle and release the god from this space.

"Wait—I think there's someone…" Demetri begins, confusion written all over his face as his eyes go distant. He tilts his head to the side, as he tries to put to words whatever it is he sees from his new powers. "I don't think this is good. I think she has—"

Without warning, a piercing squeal stabs its way through my brain, cutting off whatever it was Demetri was saying. Grasping at either side of my head, I almost lose consciousness from the pain. I don't need to hear his words to know what's happening.

Goddammit. Elira's back.

23

THREATS AND PROMISES

"*T*ake—" I sputter, trying to think, let alone form words, "her...*out*."

Dropping to my knees, I do everything I can to focus through the cacophony. I can barely tell which way is up, as I try to extend my mind beyond the excruciating interference inside my head.

There's a loud crash directly in front of me, and I can only hope it's Blake and the others going after Elira. I wouldn't know because I don't dare open my eyes.

The pain doubles down, almost as if a dial is turned up. A scream bursts from my throat and for the first time in my very long life, I wish death was an option. A true, *take-me-now*, option.

Then, as quickly as it came, the sound cuts out and peaceful silence returns to my brain.

I bend forward, resting my forehead on the floor, gasping for breath and on the verge of hurling. For the longest time, I sit there, just riding the wave of nausea and hoping it passes.

Suddenly, Blake is by my side, his warm hand on my back and his words in my ear. "Are you okay, Diana?"

Releasing my head, I stand up to witness what must be the tail end of a god intervention. Apollo glows a bright, crystalline white that pulses with a kind of power I've never witnessed.

A few feet away, risen off the floor like a cross-less Christ, is the woman with the power to manipulate sound and take me out—*Elira*. Her arms are spread out wide and her back as stiff as a board. Black and blue strands of hair float around her head as if she's been plunged into water. But what stands out most is the way her eyes are open wide, staring at nothing and everything. As the light fades around Apollo, Elira drops back to the ground. When her feet hit the floor, her legs give out, crumpling her frame into a heap.

Everyone in the room is speechless, staring at the scene with a mixture of surprise and horror.

Apollo turns to me, wiping his hands in front of him. "I believe that power should be retired. Don't you?"

"A very good call," Kyros says, nodding his approval.

"Is she—?" I begin.

"Dead?" He chuckles. "Oh, no. But I wager she'll be mad as hell when she comes back online."

"Well, it's not like I'd be sad if her lights went out permanently. What the *hell* was that?" Ren squeaks.

"Sentinel knows a lot about the supernatural community. It feels like they're small—but they have ways of understanding what makes us tick. Elira could control sound waves and she knew exactly what frequency to use on me," I say, shaking away the remnants of the audio hangover.

"You understand now, why your role is so important," Apollo says, giving me a knowing look.

"Diana, you haven't formally introduced us," Ren says, dropping his chin to his shoulder and batting his eyes. "Who is this tall, dark, and sexy man?"

"Mr. Garcia, this is the god Apollo," Kyros says. "You might wish to hold him in more reverence."

Ren practically sputters his next words. "He's th —*the* god Apollo?" His mouth hangs open and it's evident all wheels inside his head have ground to a halt.

Apollo laughs. "It's quite alright, Kyros. I am very sexy, aren't I?"

"And on that note…" I say, stepping forward. "Say goodbye to Apollo, everyone."

Renaldo, eyes still wide, raises his hand and waves with his fingers.

"Thank you for your help, Apollo. You have my deepest gratitude," I say, placing a hand on my heart. "I'm sorry I fought you so long."

A grin blossoms on his face. "Diana, I wouldn't have it any other way. You have always been the perfect fit."

"I don't know about that, but I'll do my best," I say.

He winks at me. "Pay attention to your gifts. You'll need to be one step ahead of this and I'll do whatever I can to help."

Nodding to myself I take the final step forward. I drop down to the circle and swipe my hand across the salt and chalk, creating an opening. Once the circle is broken,

Apollo's energy begins to swirl inside, until his likeness is swept away in it—vanishing into nothingness.

"Well, I don't know about you, but if working with you means being around more of that—I'm *so* in," Ren says, fanning himself.

I turn around, laughing under my breath. "And what about Brody?"

"Brody, schmody. That man was an absolute *god*."

"Literally," Blake says.

Everyone in the room laughs as relief replaces all the tension. We made it through the worst of it. Jonas is safe. Demetri has his new gift.

We're all alive.

Life is good.

"Shit. It's not over. There are three more coming. Damn, these guys are *relentless*," Demetri says, tipping his ear to the ceiling like he's a dog listening to a whistle.

"Can you figure out what they are?" I ask.

Demetri scratches the side of his temple, his eyes going distant. "Two men and one woman, I think. God, this gift is wiggy." He shakes his head, narrowing his gaze. "If I'm reading this right, one of the guys can teleport or phase in and out of locations, so be careful. The woman can manipulate energy—I think she uses it as a form of energetic binding."

"Like Wonder Woman's Golden Lasso," Jonas says, nodding. "Yeah, I remember feeling her presence. Watch out for her because she's sneaky. I was scared to death she'd come and take me."

My head whips around.

Oh, hell, no. No one is going to one-up *Diana* me.

Demetri runs a hand over his mouth, then sighs. "The other guy—he can move objects with his mind. Watch out for him. He tends to go for sharp objects." He casts his gaze to the littering of glass shards on the floor. "They're not far out."

"We need to move this fight outside," Blake says. "Ren and Kyros, take the Fletchers somewhere safe. Demetri, do you have a basement? Something without windows?"

Demetri nods. "Hell, I'll do you one better. I have a bunker downstairs."

I look over my shoulder at him, raising my eyebrows. "This is news."

"When was the last time you came over here?" Demetri counters.

"Fair point."

It's probably been a good two years since I was here last and really dug into what Demetri's been up to. But with his survivalist mentality, I'm not surprised at all that he's been hard at work.

Blake tips his head. "Show them, then meet us outside. Diana, you're with me. We'll need your insights until Demetri's back. Ren, Kyros—as much I find your style of fighting highly entertaining, stay with the Fletchers."

Ren raises his arm in the air, like he was about to snap, but doesn't. "You don't have to tell me twice. Let's get outta here, Socrates." He grabs the back of Kyros's t-shirt pushing him toward the door.

"My name's not—" Kyros begins.

"Oh for godsake, I *know*. Go with it," Ren mutters, shaking his head. "It's called humor."

Demetri walks out in front, leading the Fletchers and

the other two from the living room. "The doorway to the basement is off the kitchen. Come on."

"Let's shut this down and send a message to this Sentinel group, shall we?" Blake says, shooting me a look of total determination and confidence.

Damn, he's sexy when he takes charge.

"Let's do it," I say, straightening my shoulders and following after him.

As we exit the building, I almost miss the steps as my vision is consumed by a glimpse into the future.

"Blake, the man who teleports will be with the woman —they're coming from the back. The other one, the telekinetic man, he'll be coming at us from the front," I say as soon as the vision pulls back.

"Then out front is where we need to be," he says, grabbing his concealed pistol from the front of his jeans.

Reaching out, I place a hand over his. "I don't think we'll need that. With their powers, it could end up getting one of us hurt instead," I say.

Blake shoots me a concerned look but holsters the gun. "All right."

Before we have a chance to say anything else, the telekinetic man comes into view. He walks down the sidewalk like he's simply out for a late afternoon stroll. But I know better… I've seen glimpses of his face in my mind.

"That's him," I whisper.

Blake nods, leaning against the rail of the steps. "Understood."

I close my eyes, pushing my abilities out a few minutes into the future. "He's going to ask about Elira. Once he realizes she's inside, the guy with teleportation will be beside him. He's going to try to take us off guard. When our backs are to the men, the woman will try to slip inside."

"Then you stay here. Make sure she doesn't get past you. When Demetri comes, tell him to guard the back door," he says through the side of his mouth.

I nod in acknowledgment.

"Hi, guys," the man says, shooting us an easy smile meant to disarm us. "Have you been out here a while?"

Blake simply stares at the guy, assessing him, likely paying attention to the way he holds himself and searching for weak spots.

When neither of us answers him, he clears his throat. "I'm looking for a friend. She's about yay high. Black hair with bright blue streaks in it."

I shake my head and shrug. "Sorry, I haven't seen anyone like that."

The guy narrows his eyes. "You sure?"

"You calling me a liar?" I fire back.

"Well, she was meant to visit the guy in that house," he says, his face now stoic.

"Is that so?" Demetri says, stepping out of the building. "Well, I'm the guy who lives here and my friend here just said she hasn't seen anyone like that."

Without any more verbal banter, the guy makes his first move. His eyes take in the busted-out window and he steps forward, widening his stance. With his arms outstretched, he pulls the entire front face of the house off the building.

Demetri's eyes widen, but Blake's already in motion.

He moves like a cat, lethal in his agility. Before the guy can do much else, Blake tackles him to the ground.

"Go guard the back door," I warn, pointing behind Demetri.

"But the wall—" he says, pointing.

"We have this end covered. Just protect the back until the woman's flushed this way," I say.

"Got it." Demetri turns on his heel, rushing back through the house.

The guy kicks Blake off from him, just as the other guy teleports to the front yard. I'm ready for him, though, having seen where he pops up. Grabbing Demetri's garden rake, I swing it hard. It finds purchase right upside the guy's head and he drops like a marionette whose strings were cut.

Rushing forward, I watch as Blake and the other guy roll across the front lawn in an attempt for each to gain the upper hand.

Sirens blare to life and instantly I know that Dan and his team are on their way. It's great news, but it opens up a blind spot in the back. Leaving Blake, I rush to the back-yard, knowing that if the woman hears the sirens, she's going to rabbit.

Sure enough, I catch a glimpse of her just as realization flashes across her golden eyes. Without stopping to think, I push myself forward, running as fast as my legs will carry me.

Demetri's out the door, a few steps behind me, but he's got no chance of catching her.

As she reaches for his back gate, I dive at her feet, bring her down to the ground.

She screams like a banshee as I roll her over. Without thinking, I wind up, slapping her hard across the face. I've seen what happens when people punch each other and I like my hand intact, *thanks*.

For a moment, she stops screaming, but when the shock wears off, the scream resumes.

"Shut up," I command.

She wiggles around, trying to get out from under me. Her continual scream makes it incredibly difficult to keep my cool. My head is already aching from Elira, there's no way in hell I'm gonna let this chick make it worse.

Arching forward, she headbutts me right in the nose. Stars consume my vision and then absolute red. Despite myself, I rear up, punching her hard across her cheek-bone. Her head whips to the side in the momentum and finally, she stops her squeals.

"Holy shit, I didn't know you could hit like that," Demetri says, amusement playing at his tone.

I shoot him an agitated look and return my gaze to the women beneath me. Blood trickles from my nose and I wipe it away with the back of my hand.

"Tell whoever sent you—Jonas doesn't have his powers anymore. They're gone for good, so he better be left alone," I say, staring into her eyes.

The woman spits in my face. "We don't take kindly to threats."

"That's okay because neither do I. You've attacked me and my friends. And now, I'm coming for all of you," I say, channeling the power of Apollo, as his essence rides the wave of my words.

24

TEAM MEETING

*E*veryone sits at the circular outdoor table in the back garden of Inner Sanctum. Ren, Kyros, and Demetri stare at me expectantly, a hint of anxiety permeating the spaces between them. Blake, on the other hand, knows full-well what I'm about to tell everyone since we talked about it in depth last night. He's the only one here who looks at ease with being called here at this hour. Especially after everything that went down yesterday.

Thanks to Apollo, my life has altered its trajectory and that means making some adjustments across the board. I'm no longer able to sit by on the sidelines, using my gifts for parlor tricks and keeping old ladies happy.

It's time to play a *bigger game.*

The only way to make it all happen seamlessly is by getting everyone on the same page.

"Thank you all for coming this morning," I say, exhaling my trepidation. "I'm sure you'd all like to be doing other things, but I think we need to clear the air.

Detective Radovich was supposed to be here, too, but looks like he must have better things to do."

Blake snickers, but covers it up by rubbing at his nose. He's never been a huge fan of the Helena PD, but I'd like to think that after the past few days, he can at least see Dan's potential. Having someone inside the police department could be important down the road—and you don't need to be psychic to see that.

"Sorry I'm late," Dan says, entering the back garden through the gate behind me. He tiptoes down the cobblestone walkway, rushing past me, and taking a seat beside Kyros. He tips his chin, casting his gaze around the table, before turning his attention in my direction.

Kyros waves, his hand flapping around wildly.

"As I was saying," I say, quirking an eyebrow, *"thank you for being here."*

Dan smiles in apology. "Sorry, it's been a helluva long night processing the newbies. I haven't even been home yet. Turns out it's a lot harder to keep the supernatural criminals in check. They're slippery and seem to have innumerable resources. Turns out, it takes a lot just to keep them from posting bail and scattering."

"Have they been able—" I begin, suddenly concerned.

Dan shakes his head. "No, not yet. But I suspect they're not going to stop. We need to be prepared for a fight."

I nod. "And that's why I called you all here. There's no easy way to say it, but it needs to be said. Sentinel is going to be a problem—a *big* problem—in the future. I've seen things…" My words fade out as I think back to the insights that have been trickling in. Shuddering, I return my gaze to Blake, who nods in encouragement. "My mission is changing. I'm no longer going to be doing readings."

Ren gasps, fanning himself. "I knew it. I *knew* it. I'm out of a job. God help me."

I roll my eyes. "Oh, shut up. You're not out of a job. If anything, you're going to be more integral."

"Wait—what?" he says, his hand ceasing its movement as he leans forward.

"She said you've still got your job," Kyros says, raising his voice as if Ren was deaf.

I pinch the bridge of my nose. "Yes, Ren, you still have a job. In fact, you're being promoted to co-owner and manager."

"I'm sorry..." His eyelashes flutter. "Can you repeat that?"

Maybe he *is* deaf.

I clasp my hands into prayer position, hoping to bring in some god-essence to make it through this meeting without abandoning the whole thing and killing people instead.

"Yes, with everything I see coming, I need you here to keep Inner Sanctum going. I know you'll take good care of it, regardless of what I'm doing," I say.

"Are you leaving?" Ren asks, his voice squeaking.

I shake my head. "No—nothing like that. But this thing with Sentinel...it's going to trump everything else. And there are times when I know it will take me from here. I can't ease into my new role if I'm constantly worried about the store. With you, I know it will be in good hands."

Renaldo beams, pressing his right palm across his

heart. "Oh, my god. You aren't the cold-hearted bitch we all thought you were. See, Mr. Tightpants is doing you some good already."

Blake snickers, shaking his head and not even looking over at Ren.

"Kyros, you are going to be my go-between. You're my eyes and ears and I'll need you to be flexible in whatever comes our way," I say.

Goodness knows he comes in handy in his own way and for whatever reason, Apollo is hellbent on having him be a part of this mission. Gods help us all.

Kyros puffs up his chest, standing up from his chair. In the motion, he bumps the table, causing it to practically tip over. His chair, on the other hand, gets stuck in a groove of cobblestone and he practically lands on top of Dan.

"Whoa, easy there," Dan mutters, holding out his arms and helping Kyros stay upright.

Demetri just turns a flattened stare in my direction. "You sure know how to pick a team."

Blake huffs a laugh and jabs a thumb toward Demetri. "I'm with him."

I hang my head in defeat.

We are so doomed.

"So, what about me, then?" Demetri says. "I presume I'll be using these new gifts to help out."

I glance up from under my eyebrows. "Yes."

He nods, smiling smugly as he extends his arms out wide, so they rest on the backs of Ren and Blake's chairs.

Blake leans forward, placing his elbows on his knees, waiting.

Turning to Dan, I shoot him a sweet smile. "Detective, your role is going to be fairly obvious as well. We need a guy on the PD who can help us when things get sticky. And you know they will at times."

Dan nods. "I can see that."

"But you better damn well know that we won't be following the same protocols you do," Blake counters, shooting him a knowing look.

Dan raises his hands. "Hey, as long as I know nothing, I…know…" he narrows his gaze, "*nothing.*"

"That was profound. The Helena PD, everyone." Demetri chuckles.

"Regardless, I'm invested in this. Whatever this Sentinel group is up to, I want to make sure they don't get their way. Any people or groups that are willing to kidnap kids to get what they want—yeah, we're not friendly," Dan says, ignoring the jab.

"Here, here," Kyros says, tapping his fingertips on the table like a drum roll.

Ren rolls his eyes. "We really should have had drinks prepared for this talk. There's too much crazy going on there to be sober. Next time we have a staff meeting, I'm in charge of the setup."

I laugh. "Fair enough."

"What about '*Mr. Tightpants*' here," Demetri says, quirking an eyebrow sardonically.

The chatter ceases and the whole table goes silent.

Blake's head turns slowly toward Demetri as a low rumble escapes his chest. "It's *Blake.*"

"Gentlemen," I warn, invoking a bit of my own dominance into this mix, "let's stay on task here."

Blake sits up straighter, crossing his right ankle over his knee and exerting his dominance over his chair. Demetri gets the hint, pulling his arm back over to his side.

"Blake's here for the same reason Dan is—only he can do what the detective can't. If shit goes sideways, he's not afraid to do what it takes to get the job done. We need that. Plus, he's bound to protect me, so...*there's that*," I say, shooting him a smirk.

"And he's also her reincarnated husband, Anastasios," Kyros proudly proclaims, puffing up his chest.

All four men turn slowly to face Kyros.

"Say that again?" Demetri says, his gray eyes wide with surprise.

"Well, that was another doozy I wasn't aware of," Ren says, his eyebrows practically in his hairline. "Is there any other little secrets we should be aware of? You're not pregnant with his long-lost baby from god only knows how long ago, are you?"

I shake my head, giving him a look like he just grew horns. "No."

"Sweet baby Jesus, thank the lord," Ren counters. "I knew we needed drinks. Christ, we can't have a simple conversation anymore. All I wanted to know is if the two of you have *finally* gotten down and dirty and this is what I get." His face lightens up as a lightbulb goes off in his head. "So, if you were married to him before... Does that mean you—"

"And on that note," I say, cutting him off. I know exactly what trail his mind is going down and I need to put the kibosh on that before he gets going off on one.

"Are we all in agreement? We're in this to take down Sentinel. Ren, your first task is going to be to rearrange the way we do business. Hire some new people if you need to. I'm sure we can get some other readers or aura photographers or something in here. Hell, start some classes if you want. Just fill up the space and keep the Inner Sanctum going. It will be my cover."

"On it," he says, then stops with wide eyes. "Oh, god. Mrs. Kaminski."

Demetri chuckles. "Is that old hag hounding you guys, too? Haven't you learned yet you can just tell her that her dead pet of the week is with her and that she wants her to get a new pet?"

Ren turns to him looking scandalized. "What?"

Demetri shrugs. "Yeah, she's really just looking for permission to get a new critter. Her husband hates animals, but if she comes back saying her dead dog, cat, rabbit, robin—*whatever*—wants her to move on and get a new pet, after a while, he can't fight it. He just gives in and you have some blissful quiet for a while."

Ren's face goes distant. "Oh, I could even do that."

Demetri nods. "Right?"

I chuckle under my breath. The only reason I kept seeing Mrs. Kaminski was to watch Ren get all riled up. It was often the high entertainment for the week. Well, when my life was full of never-ending monotony. Those days are long gone.

"Well, is that us done then?" Demetri says, rubbing his hands together. "Because I could use something to eat. Who wants to come with me?"

"Oh, I would," Kyros says, raising his hand and trying to stand up.

Demetri's eyes wide and he sputters, "*Anyone* else?"

"Oh, twist my arm," Ren mutters, pushing his chair back and standing up. "I'll go, too."

Demetri turns to look at Dan, who shakes his head. "Nah, I gotta head home for some rest. I'm not as young as I used to be. Pulling an all-nighter is not my idea of a good time. Thanks, though."

Dan pushes his chair out and walks over to me. "Diana, thanks for including me as part of your team. I don't quite know what I've gotten myself into all of this, but I feel like I belong. So, thank you."

I shoot him a lopsided grin and pat him on the arm. "Anytime, Dan. Thank you for all of your help."

He tips his head, going back out of the garden the way he came.

"And what about you two?" Demetri says, raising an eyebrow. "You gonna take one for the team?"

"Actually, I think we'll pass," Blake says, extending a hand out to me.

I pull up short, surprised. "We will?"

At first, I can't help but think this is some sort of male power play, but then I see the look on Blake's face. His dimple shines triumphantly and my heart flutters in response. Whatever he wants to do, I'll follow that smile anywhere.

"Yeah. I think it's time we finally get that date of ours. Don't you?" he says, taking my hand in his.

25

IMMORTAL

"*W*here are you taking me?" I chuckle.

We've been walking around the streets of Helena in circles, with seemingly no direction in mind.

"You promise you're not looking into my head?" Blake asks, smirking.

I shake my head. "I try not to when it's unnecessary. You know that."

His grin broadens. "Good, then close your eyes."

"What?" I snicker softly. "Why?"

"Do you trust me? Or don't you?" he chides. His entire demeanor radiates playfulness and I know that whatever he has planned will likely end up being fun. Or at the very least, exciting.

My heart skips a few beats and I inhale deeply, closing my eyes. "Fine."

"Excellent. Keep them closed, okay?" he says, grabbing hold of my hand. With a gentle tug, he leads me forward. "I'll let you know when we're there."

"All right." I have to actively work at not picking up on

his plans because of our physical connection and the fact that it must be in the forefront of his mind.

We walk in silence for a few moments, as I put all of my energy into making sure I don't trip over my own two feet. The sidewalks of Helena aren't known for their levelness, after all.

"I must look ridiculous, you know," I say, fighting the urge to open my eyes.

"Since when do you care what others think of you?" Blake asks, his words resonating with a knowing well beyond this lifetime's connection together. It goes straight to the heart of who we are together—*to our bond.*

"Fair." I nod, unable to challenge that one.

"Don't worry, your wait is almost over. We're nearly there," he says, laughing.

Despite myself, my mind rolls through the different places he could be taking me in our small town. There's only a couple of locations I can think of within walking distance. The small diner I go to practically every day, the park in the middle of town, the trails that lead down to the river, and the smattering of small shops. Beyond that, there isn't much. We don't even have a bowling alley or movie theater.

Suddenly, we stop moving.

Blake's breath is hot against the skin of my neck as he whispers in my ear, "Okay, you can open your eyes."

Smiling to myself, my eyelids flutter open. Instantly, I feel like kicking myself.

Of course, it would be here.

"Ruby Moon Coffee Shop?" I say. It's not a question, but it still comes out as one.

Blake drops my hand, splaying his arms out wide. "Hey, I did promise to get a true date at the coffee shop. Did I not? And since all of our other plans have fallen through, I figured it must be a sign."

My eyebrows rise. "A *sign*, huh. Have I converted you into a believer, now, Mr. Wilson?"

He grins broadly, his dimple casting a deep grooves beside his goatee. "I think I still need a little convincing." His eyes twinkle mischievously as he tips his head toward the door.

Stepping forward, he reaches out and opens it up. He stands aside, ushering me in first.

Tipping my head, I step forward and walk into the coffee shop. Maxwell, the owner stands behind the bar, along with a teenage barista I've never seen before.

Guilt rolls through me as I see him, because the last time I was here, I was kind of a bitch to Max.

Sucking it up, I hold my head high and walk up to the counter, ready to place my order.

Max shakes his head. "I'm not taking your order."

I pull up short, shooting him a look of annoyance. "Come on, Max. I know I was a bit abrupt last time—"

He makes a face, shaking his hand, and warding me off from continuing, "I don't give two shits about that. I just mean you're already taken care of."

Confusion creeps through me and he raises his right hand, pointing behind me.

I turn around, realizing there's not a single person besides us in the coffee shop. Blake stands beside the booth we shared before, and an entire spread of goodies is laid out across the table.

The teenage barista, waltzes over to the door, her brown ponytail bopping back and forth in the movement. With a flick of her wrist, she locks the door and flips the sign from *open* to *closed*.

My eyebrows tug in and I take a tentative step toward Blake. "What's all this?"

"This," Blake says, extending his hand toward the table, "is our *official* first date."

My heart flutters, reminding me that even after all the years of disappointment and heartache, it still beats. It's still ready to be handed over to him.

I tip my head, walking over to the booth and sliding into my seat. As soon as I'm in, he sits down beside me, shoving me over with his ass, and forcing me closer to the wall. The warmth of his leg pulses through my pant leg and I inhale sharply.

Being together hasn't been easy. From the very beginning, two millennia ago, it was hard. But even now that we have our lives back—it's been incredibly difficult to get two minutes alone.

"So, how did you pull all of this off?" I ask, narrowing my gaze. Even if I wanted to, I couldn't wipe the smile from my face. I pick up the cup of coffee with whip cream and tiny marshmallows on top—clearly it's mine.

Blake places his palm on my thigh, grinning. "I have my ways." He grabs his cup of black coffee, and takes a sip.

"Ren helped you, didn't he?" I say, wiping the whipped cream from my face and grabbing a small scone.

For a moment, a hint of panic flashes across his features. "I thought you said you'd stay out—"

"No, it was just an educated guess." I laugh, breaking off a bite from the scone and popping it into my mouth.

"Ah," he exhales, sinking back into his seat a bit. "Well, he had other things in mind, but I had to put the kibosh on that. He's certainly...*colorful*. At least, with his date ideas."

"Do *not* take dating tips from Ren, please," I say, trying to pull back the expression that gives away the absolute terror creeping through me.

Blake snickers. "Duly noted."

I exhale, scooting another inch closer, and placing my head on his shoulder. "I want this to be about you and me rediscovering each other. As we are."

He turns to me, planting a kiss on the top of my head. His right hand extends out, brushing a chunk of my pink hair behind my ear. "Then it shall be done."

I sigh in complete and utter content. Even with all of the craziness—Sentinel, the drama, new missions... I wouldn't want to be anywhere but here, right now. In this moment.

Then, without warning, I'm pulled from the coffee shop and placed in the middle of a graveyard in a prophetic vision. Snow blows across the landscape, making me shiver.

Transplanted somewhere in the future, I look around, trying to get my bearings. Off in the distance, a man and woman get out of a vehicle and walk over to the columbarium. I can't make out a word they say, but it doesn't matter.

Whatever they're saying isn't what's important.

Instead, they stop talking, making their way around

the side of the building, only to stumble back. A man—*if you can call him that*—surges forward. His clothes are tattered and his skin is falling from his face as if he's seen the better side of death and should be sent back there. STAT.

The woman screams and the man takes her hand, trying to direct her away from the zombie-like creature, only to be faced with another one. This one was a woman at one point and has scary-fast reflexes for a dead chick.

I lunge forward, my arms extended. Yet, as soon as I make a move to react, I'm pulled from the scene and shoved into the middle of a bedroom.

The lights are low, but in the center of the room is a young man with cropped black hair and dark skin. He's sitting on the edge of a bed, his elbows on his knees as he clutches at a photograph.

From this angle, it's hard to make out, but the tears streaming down his cheek are enough to endear me to him. He's hurting, that much is certain, but I don't know why. It's like his feelings aren't clear, even to him.

Stepping forward, I reach out, placing an ethereal hand on his shoulder. As soon as I do, I'm thrust from the bedroom and into a cavern of some sort.

The lights are dim, but the energy is insanely malevolent. Something is not right and there's a power rising that could level the whole area if it's released.

All the hairs on my body rise—even though I'm acutely aware this is a vision and my body isn't actually here.

The word "*Fetch*" comes to mind, though I have absolutely no context for it.

Am I supposed to play a game? Like a dog?

"What is this?" I call out, trying to pull the threads of whatever is sending me this insight. "Apollo, if this is you, I need more to go on. It's too cryptic."

Suddenly, I'm consumed by an overwhelming sense of dread. It's soul-crushing—like the *end* is inevitable.

Again, the scene shifts, and I'm left in a vehicle with two kids. Blake is at the wheel but in the backseat is the same boy from the bedroom and a young woman of about the same age.

His...*sister*?

The knowing comes to be without searching for it.

They're twins. And not just any kind, either.

Gemini Twins.

I've heard of Gemini Twins through passing, but even in all my years, never had the opportunity to cross their paths.

"Help them," the words rise into my consciousness before I see who speaks them.

The vision of the car ride gives way to the mountainside of Parnassus. It's his favorite, after all.

Apollo walks into view, his dark curls tousling in the wind. "Help them," he repeats.

"Who are they? How do I help them?" I say, exhaling the dread from moments before.

"Prepare for an extended leave. Go to Windhaven Connecticut when the time is right. You'll see the signs," he says. "It's *imperative* they get reeled in. The future of everything depends on it."

"Are they a danger? Is that what I'm sensing?" I ask.

"Only if left unchecked. They need your guidance and protection. Help them, Diana. You're the only one who can," he says, vanishing into the breeze that tousled his hair.

Then, once again, I'm back in the coffee shop, still in the booth besides Blake. His arms are wrapped around me and the teenager behind the coffee bar is screaming.

"What was that? Did you see that?" she wails.

I don't have the strength to even acknowledge her. Instead, I lean into Blake, taking a deep breath through my nose to center myself.

Something terrible is coming...

"What is it? What did you see?" Blake says, his voice wavering.

Swallowing hard, I open my eyes and sit up. "I saw…" I shake my head, still fighting back the absolute terror that permeated every cell of my body when I was in the cavern. "Something dreadful is coming and I need to…"

My words cut off as I try to recall the two kids in my mind, burning them into my memory.

They're so young—maybe Aidan's age. Maybe less.

How can they possibly be a threat to everyone?

And what does that have to do with the zombies?

"Diana?" Blake says, urging me on.

"Why does everything have to be so cryptic? You'd think with as powerful as my gifts are, I'd have more of the answers," I say, shaking my head.

"Maybe Apollo knows you still need a bit of a mystery to get you moving?" he offers.

I lean back in my seat. "Huh, never thought of it that way."

"So, what's going on? Fill me in." Blake's eyes are haunted as he watches me.

Here we are, on our first date, and already we can't be left alone.

I turn to the side, looking him in the eye. "We're going to be taking a road trip up north. I have our next mission from Apollo."

"Okay," Blake says, concern still painting his features. "Where?"

Shuddering from the dread still lingering at the back of my mind, I whisper, *"Windhaven."*

To be continued...

Up Next: ***Immortals:*** Book 3 in the Diana Hawthorne Supernatural Mysteries Series.
Coming December 2021

CAN'T WAIT FOR MORE DIANA?

Diana Hawthorne seems to get around. (No, not like that. Get your mind out of the gutter.)

If you're waiting for Diana's supernatural mystery series to continue, here are a few additional places you can get your fix:

The Final Five
Awakening
The Windhaven Witches

ALSO BY CARISSA ANDREWS

THE WINDHAVEN WITCHES

Secret Legacy

Soul Legacy

Haunted Legacy

Cursed Legacy

THE PENDOMUS CHRONICLES

Trajectory: A Pendomus Chronicles Prequel

Pendomus: Book 1 of the Pendomus Chronicles

Polarities: Book 2 of the Pendomus Chronicles

Revolutions: Book 3 of the Pendomus Chronicles

THE 8TH DIMENSION NOVELS

The Final Five: An *Oracle & Awakening* Bridge Novelette

Awakening: Rise as the Fall Unfolds

Love is a Merciless God

ABOUT THE AUTHOR

Carissa Andrews
Sci-fi/Fantasy is my pen of choice.

 Carissa Andrews is an international bestselling indie author from central Minnesota who writes a combination of science fiction, fantasy, and dystopia. Her plans for 2021 include continuation of her Diana Hawthorne Supernatural Mysteries. As a publishing powerhouse, she keeps sane by chilling with her husband, five kids, and their two insane husky pups, Aztec and Pharaoh.

For a free ebook and to find out what Carissa's up to, head over to her website and sign up for her newsletter: www.carissaandrews.com

facebook.com/authorcarissaandrews

twitter.com/CarissaAndrews

instagram.com/carissa_andrews_mn

amazon.com/author/carissaandrews

bookbub.com/authors/carissa-andrews

goodreads.com/Carissa_Andrews

Made in the USA
Coppell, TX
23 January 2022